# Witch-Cult Abbey

# Witch-Cult Abbey

## Mark Samuels

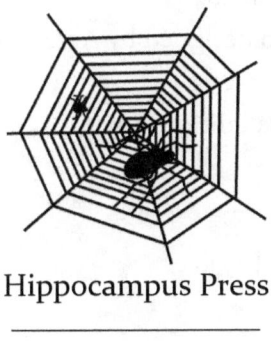

Hippocampus Press

New York

Published by Hippocampus Press
P.O. Box 641, New York, NY 10156.
www.hippocampuspress.com

First published by Zagava, 2020.
Hippocampus Press logo designed by Anastasia Damianakos.

First Hippocampus Press Edition, 2021
1 3 5 7 9 8 6 4 2

ISBN 978-1-61498-352-1

# Chapter One

I have sometimes amused myself by endeavouring to fancy what
would be the fate of any individual gifted, or rather accursed,
with an intellect *very* far superior to that of his race . . . This subject is a painful one indeed. That such individuals *have* so soared
above the plane of their race, is scarcely to be questioned; but, in
looking back through history for traces of their existence, we
should pass over all biographies of "the good and the great" while
we search carefully the slight records of wretches who died in
prison, in Bedlam, or upon the gallows.—EDGAR A. POE

When the air-raid warning sounded I awoke from a dream of a
vast, labyrinthine abbey, of shelves stuffed with long-
mouldering volumes, and of a lost, mist-wreathed rural landscape bathed in moonlight and darkness. For a few moments I
was caught between two worlds, unable to determine which
was the more real, but as that drone persisted, its sound drove
all other considerations from my mind. I reached out to the
nightstand and put on my spectacles. From below I could hear
Mrs Cooper shouting up the stairs for me to join her and her
husband and get to the Anderson Shelter in the back garden. I
clambered out of bed in the darkness, slipped a dressing gown
over my pyjamas, and limped barefoot towards the door, fumbling for the cane propped against the inside jamb.

On the landing the blur of objects I had seen hundreds of
times before now seemed unfamiliar; vague outlines of pictures
and potted plants rendered alien by the shadows. Mrs Cooper
cried out, "Mr Prior, do 'urry up!" and I pushed forward across
the landing to see her framed at the bottom of the stairway, fully
dressed, illuminated by the flame from the candle she held.

And when I clambered awkwardly down the stairs, crab-like, the sound of the air-raid warning was accompanied by the roar of engines and muffled explosions coming from far off.

With grumbling impatience she took me by the arm when I reached the ground floor, fairly dragging me through the kitchen and into the back garden. Once we were across the threshold she snuffed out the candle.

The Coopers had turned most of this small garden into an allotment wherein they grew—invariably—dwarfish vegetables, and it was hazardous, in the semi-darkness, to navigate through the low maze of wire and wood designed to keep off birds and other animals. At least it was hazardous for me. Mrs Cooper herself knew the correct route to take through long association. Moreover, she appeared to enjoy dragging along a stumbling half-cripple after her. I could not help but reflect upon the couple's childlessness and my status in the household.

I looked up only once to take in my surroundings, and almost lost my footing in a plot of slug-riddled cabbages.

The backs of the terraced houses were sheets of darkness in the blackout, all windows covered by thick fabric, but I could still make out the multitude of sloping roofs and chimneys against the skyline. There was a crescent, waxing moon low in the east. Searchlight beams directing the local anti-aircraft gun-sites moved slowly across the gloom, occasionally blurred by strands of thin grey cloud. The muffled gasps of bombs as they struck London seemed nearer than before, and I expected at any moment to see the red glare of incendiary fires breaking out on the horizon, but Mrs Cooper forestalled the sight by shepherding me down the short flight of wooden steps into the total blackness of the Anderson Shelter.

I heard a dog bark at me, then a yelp as it was kicked, followed by Mr Cooper's grunt of satisfaction. The man himself suddenly appeared in front of a paraffin lantern he had just re-filled and had only at that moment managed to light success-fully. The dog, Buster, a gargoyle-like terrier, sloped off into a corner and regarded me with baleful eyes as if I had dealt him the blow and not Cooper.

I cannot say I entirely welcomed the prospect of spending the duration of the air-raid in close quarters with the Coopers again. But I had already experienced the only overnight alter-native: a casual ticket at the Underground shelter at Highgate Archway Station. By six A.M., after a near-sleepless period of ten or so hours, the coughing, the furtive coupling, and the snoring became unbearable. There was also the itch of lice. The racket-eers, when selling tickets for bunks, did an additional trade in delousing powders for the morning after. One of them thought it a good idea on certain nights to keep morale up by bringing a banjo down into the depths so everyone could have a Cockney sing-along together. On other nights the local middle-class branch of London communists would be lecturing working-class folk about imperialist wars being fought for the idle rich (they ignored the hard fact of Russian troops occupying eastern Poland and Finland). The misery of such occasions was inex-pressible. I had had more than enough of subterranean "Ta-ra-ra-boom-de-ays" or else attempted renditions of "The Red Flag" and "The Internationale."

It was another world entirely. The whole city above could have been flattened and no one would have been any the wiser down there. At least here, in the company of the Coopers, de-spite its corrugated iron cocoon of the Anderson Shelter, and even with layers of soil on top, one was not entirely cut off from the world. Mr Cooper had rigged the wireless set to work inside the shelter with a huge battery and outside aerial.

Yet even in this refuge there was a regular routine. I knew it off by heart.

Ten minutes into the air-raid and Mr Cooper opened the first bottle of Navy Rum. He produced some tin cups and poured out generous measures all round. When the bottle was half-empty one of the Coopers would turn on the wireless set and the two of them, she a little more tight than he was, would start dancing in those cramped confines, probably to something by the Ray Noble Orchestra, while Buster would growl at me from the shadows.

Once the all-clear had sounded, the three of us, bleary-eyed and fuzzy from the effects of the rum, would stagger back to the two-up, two-down, terraced house and sleep off our excesses. Eventually, a few hours later, Mrs Cooper would rise first and provide us all with a breakfast of kippers, greasy tea, and porridge. Mr Cooper would wolf it down and depart for his day's work at an emporium in Camden where he laboured in a back room, ostensibly restoring secondhand furniture. My own routine would then commence: the writing of letters to various quarters in search of a desk job, a solitary luncheon at a Tufnell Park tea-shop, more letters in the afternoon, an evening in the company of well-thumbed books, a cold supper, and at the end of it sleep or inebriation, accompanied by far-off bombs.

In my case, death had stubbornly insisted upon staying its hand.

Early on in the war, during that period the papers were now describing as "phony," I had been classed as unfit for active military service on account of my half-useless right leg.

The rest of my family, incidentally, were either dead, estranged, or imbecilic. I had not seen or thought of them for years. I was left to make my way in the world alone—an outcome very much to my own satisfaction.

My single form of past employment had been as a cataloguer of antiquarian books in an establishment just off Hampstead High Street, which position I had held for little over a year until the owner had died suddenly, with the business being then sold off by the executors of his estate, leaving me surplus to requirements. I had enjoyed the work, despite being mostly confined to a windowless, book-choked storeroom that was lit only by gaslight, where dust attached itself to one's person like some ghostly paramour.

In short, I was entirely unsuited to provide worthwhile assistance to the war effort.

My sole purpose, it seemed, was to hibernate until this outbreak of leprous ideologies had played itself out across the European continent.

The letter that was to provide some form of deliverance from my bondage was very nearly torn to pieces before I had the opportunity to see it: each postal delivery drove the dog Buster to heights of territorial frenzy. He could sense in advance—by smell I supposed—the imminent arrival of the local postman and would position himself in the hallway ready to defend his patch. The Coopers had very little interest in the mail dropping through the letterbox (as far as I was aware, they had no correspondents, and any bills arriving took their own chances of survival). But for Buster, all letters were proof of enemy action and a call to arms; they were gas-bombs which dropped onto his blessed plot of land—and carried the nauseating stench of men in uniform (albeit a Royal Mail uniform in this instance). Should an urgent telegram requiring an immediate reply ever have successfully arrived at the Cooper household it would represent an affront to Buster's doggy universe.

That morning, as ever, Mrs Cooper was working on the allotment ("Dig for Victory"), and Mr Cooper had departed for the furniture emporium ("Keep Calm and Carry On"). I therefore blithely trusted in my own early-warning, tried-and-tested measures in order to thwart Buster's assault on invasive pieces of paper. From the vantage point of my upper-room window, I was able to spot the postman on the other side of the street making deliveries. His routine was such as to practically guarantee that, once spotted, I knew he would be in position outside the Cooper front door within another five minutes at most. It was then that I would go downstairs to the hall, position myself alongside Buster, and restrain him with my walking cane long enough to retrieve any communications addressed to me. (Occasionally, to keep Buster happy, I might allow him to chew on what rare mail was addressed to the Coopers.)

However, this morning the postman either varied his route or had fewer letters to deliver, so despite my spotting him beforehand, he made his arrival just as I hobbled my way towards the foot of the stairs.

I saw the envelope tumble onto the inside doormat and heard Buster's satisfied grunt of anticipation. By lunging forward with unaccustomed agility, I managed to interject my cane between him and the letter addressed to me. Buster's jaws clamped firmly on its lower shaft and he shook his head from side to side, pulling the cane from my grasp.

Buster had been too slow, though, for, in the interim, I had put the letter in my jacket pocket and the dog was baffled. He sniffed the air, barked once or twice, and then began scratching at the door, signalling his desire to be let out at once in order to hunt down the already rapidly departing postman.

"Hard luck, old fellow," I said as I retrieved my cane, wiping canine saliva from the lower portion with a handkerchief.

Buster twisted away from the door and glared at me fierce-ly—rather, I imagine, as a retired colonel might glare at a sus-pected fifth-columnist trying to pass the time of day with him at his golf club.

Back upstairs in my room, I examined the envelope. The post-mark was smeared and illegible. The unfamiliar handwriting, bearing my name and address, was in a clear copperplate style. I tore open the gummed flap and took out the missive within. It read as follows:

> Thool Abbey
> Gallows Langley
> Hertfordshire

Dear Mr Prior,

Your current address was provided to us by the estate for the late proprietor of the Hampstead Antiquarian Bookshop from which establishment our family had procured several dozen vol-umes for the abbey library. We found the book catalogues, which we are given to understand were compiled by yourself, a model of accurate, informative descriptiveness.

We currently seek to employ a respectable person from with-in the trade for a full-time position cataloguing the entire library. This would entail occupancy in the abbey for a period of two months or so.

Should you be inclined to accept the position please make yourself available in person on the 18th inst., shortly before noon, where you will be collected from Gallows Langley Railway Sta-tion.

> Yours truly,
> Lady Caroline Degabaston

I took in the letter's contents. The name Thool Abbey was vaguely known to me; it was indeed possible the bookshop's catalogues went to that unusual address. Degabaston was a blank, but then again, if she were the daughter of some bibli-

ophilic member of the nobility, and not herself the actual ad-
dressee, it might explain the situation. Billy Jenkins, the shop's
postal clerk, had been the one to address and despatch the
items ordered from the catalogue. I wondered what books had
been sent there: and was the letter actually offering me the position in advance should I choose to accept it, before any interview, and even before supplying references? It appeared
indefinite about this issue. The assumption seemed to be that
by keeping the scheduled appointment on the eighteenth of
this month I signalled my assent. Although there was no figure
for my salary cited, such is often the way, or so I understand,
within the strict traditions of aristocratic reticence in such
matters.

There was nothing realistic keeping me from an appointment at the abbey.

Surely, I thought, I should look upon it as an unexpected
stroke of possible good fortune. Perhaps that curious dream
just before I had been awoken by the air-raid siren in the early
hours had foreshadowed it. And if I was taken on, there and
then, I would have the "two months or so" in the countryside,
away from London and the bombing. If I were not taken on for
some reason, or if the financial terms offered were absurd, I
could return the same day and be none the worse off for my
experience.

A yet deeper hibernation within the library of secluded
Thool Abbey beckoned.

A few days later, on the morning of my departure, the Coopers
decided to make a terrible fuss over me.

Whether it was the loss of income my potential decamp-
ment to the countryside presented or whether they had really
come to look upon me as more than a paying lodger, I was not

sure: their first reaction to the news of my visiting Gallows Langley to follow up a "live-in" job prospect was, frankly, one of apparent bafflement I should even take it seriously. They seemed to suspect a prank.

But on the appointed day itself the Cooper staple breakfast of kippers and porridge was replaced by powdered eggs and slices of greasy bacon heaped on toasted, buttered bread. And, while we ate, the two of them began to reminisce about recent nights spent in the Anderson Shelter; about how "we had seen off the worst the Luftwaffe could throw at us"; and how it had brought the household together as a "real, proper family, like." A new lodger, they opined, "most likely just wouldn't appreciate the bond that had been forged."

I nodded politely at appropriate moments, cleared my plate, and then went upstairs to shave, wash, and change into my best suit. Looking around at the room I realised that, were I to take up temporary residency at the abbey, I would not miss it very much. I had scarcely left any mark upon it to indicate I had lived there for six dreary months: only a shelf of well-thumbed books, used soap and razors, a dingy towel, a frayed shoe-brush and polish, some grubby stationery, and just enough clothes to half-fill the single wardrobe.

When I eventually made my way downstairs, clean and smartly clad in the navy-blue suit, I saw that both the Coopers were waiting in order to see me off. He must have specially delayed his departure to the furniture emporium, while she was dabbing the watery sides of her eyes with a lace handkerchief.

I paused there awkwardly and a few words were exchanged.

"Good luck, young fella," Mr Cooper said, whilst shaking my hand.

Mrs Cooper made a move as if to peck me on the cheek, but turned away at the last moment.

"I'm not sure they'll definitely take me on," I said. "They may have other people to consider."

Both looked doubtful. In their eyes the matter was already quite settled. The notion it was all an elaborate prank seemed to have dissipated entirely. I wondered if they now thought I'd cooked the whole thing up simply as a ruse to leave; whether in fact I'd not discovered cheaper lodgings elsewhere and wished to quit them without causing offence.

"Well, I have to go if I'm to catch that train from Euston Station," I said.

They stepped to one side and I took a step forward.

Something was holding me back.

My left leg, the good one, would not budge.

I twisted around and saw Buster had his jaws fastened into the rolled-up flap of my trouser leg.

He was looking up at me with a curious expression I'd not seen before in his eyes. When Mrs Cooper eventually coaxed him free and then held him in her arms he started whining, very uncharacteristically, and kept on staring at me.

The situation was becoming absurd.

"Thanks for everything," I said. "Look, there's a good chance I'll be back here before you know it."

They said nothing, only nodded uncertainly, and I was out the front door, pushing myself forward in a hurried fluster with the aid of my cane.

As I turned into Junction Road, a number 10 double-decker appeared, whose route took in the Euston Road, and I just managed to board it at the corner stop where a number of other passengers had formed themselves into an orderly queue. There was nowhere left to sit on the lower deck of the omnibus, so I hauled myself up the turn of the stairway to the upper deck. The cloying fog of tobacco smoke tamped down the odour of all the unwashed bodies up there.

I got off at the Doric Arch outside the railway terminus, passed across the square to the ticket office, and bought a day-return on a stopping train rather than the express service to Birmingham, which bypassed Gallows Langley altogether. There was just enough time for a cup of tea before the train was scheduled to start. The waitress was prompt and efficient, so I left her the change from a bob as a tip. Given that I was dressed in my best suit, she seemed to have taken me for someone more well-off than I actually was, or perhaps she had noticed the cane. Still, it felt satisfying to be generous.

I wandered along the platform with just a few minutes left in hand, trying to find a third-class part of my train that looked relatively empty.

As I clambered aboard the guard blew his whistle.

I took off my hat, put it on the rack above, settled next to the window, and stared out at the web-like, sooty ironwork of the interior of the station's titanic roof. My cane rested across my lap. I anticipated a quiet journey.

But just as the train pulled away from the platform a group of three young men in army uniforms—two privates and a corporal—tumbled desperately into the carriage, one after the other.

They arranged themselves on the benches and looked me up and down in turns. There was obviously some discrepancy, at least in their eyes, between my attire and my travelling third-class.

"What's the stick in aid of?" one of them, a youth with beady eyes and a toothbrush moustache enquired.

The train gathered speed as it pulled out of the platform, trailing steam and smuts.

"Blind, are ya?" said another—portly, sweating—who slipped a Woodbine between his fleshy lips.

"Actually I'm—"

"*Sprechen Sie Deutsch?*" interrupted toothbrush moustache with a grin. He nudged the corporal (thin, cleft-lip) beside him, who kept tapping at his wristwatch.

"Should arsk 'im for 'is identity papers," said Woodbine.

"Do I have to call the guard?" I said.

"Only a joke, old cock," said toothbrush moustache.

"Shut up, Smith," said the corporal. "We're in enough trouble as it is. It's your fault we're in this bloody mess."

He held his watch up to his ear and began shaking his wrist back and forth.

I turned to gaze out of the window, watching as bomb-damaged London slid by.

The soldiers eventually disembarked at Watford, after which the train gradually left behind the endless metropolitan labyrinth of houses and streets. The closeted smear of concrete grey and of red-brick turned into open greenery, and the horizon was bordered by trees and not by rooftops. The odour of animal dung, rather than chimney smoke from coal fires, reached my nostrils. The countryside was bathed in late morning sunshine, and I watched fields full of sheep and cows who did not bother to look up from their contented grazing. They seemed blind and deaf to the noisy steam-rasps of the train engine and the rat-a-tat of carriage wheels rolling over the lines only some thirty or so yards away from them. They had no fear of the wider destruction wrought by the machine age.

My journey lasted for another ten or so minutes, carrying

me deeper into rural Hertfordshire until at last the train slipped into the middle of nowhere—Gallows Langley Station. I picked up and put on my hat, alighted, saw the guard at the rear waving a flag, and began, crab-like, with my cane supporting me, to make my way along the platform. The train whistled, exhaling its breath more copiously into the atmosphere, trailing a fog of smut-dotted steam as it gradually pulled away into the distance.

The platforms for the up and down lines were connected by an iron-wrought Victorian bridge for pedestrian use. On the far side, over this bridge, lay the ticket office and the entrance to (and exit from) the station. A uniformed station-master was in attendance. I was the only person to have disembarked from the service at this stop on the line. I made my way towards him, climbing and descending the bridge's twin set of stairs, conscious of the fact I could not possibly walk as quickly as would have been expected from an able-bodied passenger. Whether it was impertinence or a part of his duties as a time-keeper I had no idea, but he took out his fob-watch and glanced at it as I slowly loped closer towards him.

"Morning to you, sir," he said when I was a few yards from him. "Train's slightly late, I see. Still, better than not at all, eh?"

I patted my outside pockets.

"Lost your ticket?"

I went through all my pockets this time, without finding the thing. Just as I was about to apologise, another figure appeared behind the station-master, having emerged from the depths of the ticket office. The figure was elderly, bony, dressed wholly in black, and wore a wide-brimmed church-warden's hat. I was immediately struck by a certain marked irregularity in his wizened facial features, as if the mouth, eyes, and nose were off-centre, even to the extent of being lopsided.

His skin was shockingly pale, like that of a stranger to sunlight, and his left eye was very bloodshot.

"Mr Prior is expected at the abbey," the apparition said.

"Are you Mr Prior?" the station-master asked me.

"Yes, I am."

"Well, that's quite all right then, sir, I'll let you pass."

The person sent to collect me from the station was, I supposed, one of a retinue of ancient retainers in the employ of Lady Degabaston. He did not introduce himself but silently escorted me to a horse and trap waiting in the narrow lane nearby. Little more than a dirt-track, it climbed a steep hill in a direction leading away from the railway line and directly into the countryside.

I did not question this bony myrmidon, for there seemed nothing requiring explanation. He stiffly climbed up to the front bench and I followed, awkwardly, eventually seating myself beside him. He flicked the reins and the horse moved forward. The beast did not seem to me, at first glance, to be well suited to easily master the upwards gradient that lay ahead of it; but it must have possessed keen reserves of strength and stamina, for the ascent along the rutted yet uneven course ahead was undertaken without so much as a single pause in the muffled, regular thumping of its hooves.

The effect of this rhythm made me feel drowsy, despite my trepidation at the prospect of the interview with Lady Degabaston still to come. I felt half-hypnotized in some unaccountable fashion, and what came next was perceived in the manner of half-awakening from sleep.

The watery sun had given up the ghost and was finally obscured by a continuous sheet of slate-grey cloud that had risen over the horizon. The light grew dimmer and hordes of stunted, tortuously branched trees pressed upon us from both sides.

Ahead, on the crest of the hill, I saw a signpost, painted in black and white, but almost swallowed up by tenacious ivy, bearing the directions "To the Station, 1 Mile" and "To the Abbey, 5 miles."

And once we had reached the summit there was a clear view ahead down across a depopulated valley. A low, shifting ground-mist had moored itself there in semi-permanent occupancy, there was a patchwork of fields and woodlands through which meandered a sinuous river the colour of tainted silver, and, at the heart of this crepuscular region, the abbey itself dominated the landscape.

We descended directly into the valley of Thool.

The abbey disappeared and reappeared as we wound our way towards it, blotted out by now higher tree-lines of curiously misshapen oaks but then seen again in the distance across a succession of empty, untended fields. With each fleeting glimpse, I had the weird feeling that the building was drawing itself closer to me, rather than me drawing closer to it.

But at last we reached the grounds of the estate.

The horse and trap passed through an open trellis-work gateway where red-lichen dappled gargoyles bearing curious snouts hunched on twin stone pillars, and we travelled down a long drive flanked by untended weed-riddled lawns, while the morbidly oppressive bulk of the abbey reared up immediately ahead.

The frontage, with its crenellated turret and imposing portico (surely both later additions), was half-choked by creeping ivy, as if time sought to mask its transformation from a place of worship into a secular dwelling-house. The original structure was not built on the scale of other, greater abbeys, such as Tintern or Glastonbury; it was a dwarfish architectural cousin: one that had escaped the full force of the sixteenth-century dissolutions and suppressions and, therefore, had not finally been left to vacancy. At this moment, of course, its actual history was unknown to me, though I suspected that its survival, intact, indicated that whatever monkish order had occupied the site had submitted freely to Henry the Eighth's imperious demand that he be recognised as the supreme head of the Church in England. At some later stage, probably in the reign of Elizabeth the First, the monks must have nevertheless been wholly assimilated into the established church and been made to marry, or else been exposed, like all the others, to contempt and beggary for continued Romish adherence.

I had felt an acute sensation of nausea and loathing when we had pulled up outside the entrance portico, the horse still neighing and steaming after its exertions; but I nevertheless allowed the bony myrmidon to take my arm, help me alight, and then ferry me, lest I stagger, across the threshold and into the gloomy interior of Thool Abbey.

# Chapter Two

I have made my bed
In charnels and on coffins, where black death
Keeps record of the trophies won from thee,
Hoping to still these obstinate questionings
Of thee and thine, by forcing some lone ghost
Thy messenger, to render up the tale
Of what we are.
　　　　　—PERCY BYSSHE SHELLEY, *Alastor* (1816)

That acute sense of nausea left me in a daze, and I took in my surroundings with a self-distracted vagueness—an imposing entrance hall, a central staircase sweeping in an arc to a balcony above, walls panelled in cracked mahogany dating back centuries, frayed Persian rugs and antiquated furniture dotted here and there in confusing profusion. Dust and cobwebs prevailed over cleanliness. The air itself was musty with decay and neglect.

I could scarcely catch my breath and, freeing myself from the steadying arm of the servant (who still had not spoken), I slumped into a chair to try and recover my composure.

"Where is your mistress?" I managed to say to him after a moment or two. "Is she not awaiting my arrival? I thought I was here to be interviewed."

"So you will be," he replied. "All in good time. There is refreshment laid out for you in the library—after your long journey, sir."

The thought of my being able to keep anything down at this moment was a fantastical notion.

My discomfort seemed apparent to him.

"It is nothing. The sensation will soon pass," he said. "It is not uncommon at first. The library is through the low arched door opposite, on your far left. You will excuse me: I have to stable the horse, sir."

He inclined his head slightly and then drifted away, leaving me alone.

I again tried to recover my composure; but after several minutes had elapsed and the worst of the nausea had abated, I finally felt able to get to my feet. Leaning heavily on my cane, I made my way across the expanse of the hall, through the door he had indicated, and into the library. This long, vaulted chamber must also once have formed the abbey's scriptorium. The handwritten productions of its monks—and sundry incunabula—had apparently long since been removed, as the shelves on the interior wall were now occupied by irregularly laid-out and disorderly rows of rebound volumes. Overspill contents had been piled up at the bases of the shelves and left to accumulate capriciously. A series of arched, latticed windows, nestled between columns of untidy bookshelves on the inside of the external wall, admitted a grey, late-morning light.

It would be, I thought, a mammoth undertaking to accomplish organisation and cataloguing of the volumes in just two months.

What of the surroundings?

Could I bear it? What choice had I?

I had borne the gaslit basement choked with volumes, that dungeon in which I had laboured for months when employed by the Hampstead bookshop.

I picked up one of the volumes at random and opened it. The following lines caught my eye:

*"Do the dead speak a language whose meaning contains all possible meanings since their mode of being is outside space and time?"*

It appeared to be nothing more than a book of gibberish, and I replaced it on the shelf.

On a central table were the refreshments the servant said had been laid out for me. My nausea had now wholly passed, and I felt able to think about consuming something—for I had not eaten since breakfast, hours ago. What was offered, however, was not appetising: slices of bread cut from a brown loaf with some kind of half-cooked pink meat as a filling, a bowl of salt, and a small glass of bitter-tasting red wine. I left it all mostly untouched.

I took out my pocket-watch to discover it had stopped working, despite my having wound it last night as usual. It had stopped some time after my arrival at Gallows Langley Station and showed the hour, wrongly, as ten minutes past eleven. I wound it again, but to no avail: the thing remained silent and refused to tick. By my own reckoning I must have already been seated in the library for half an hour. Taking into account the additional journey from the station to Thool Abbey, it must already be close to one o'clock in the afternoon. So much for the instruction I arrive before midday. There was no sign of the servant. I waited another fifteen minutes or so until I could no longer bear the suspense. I had no idea if it was a breach of etiquette to go in search of an explanation, but I did so nevertheless.

There was no one in the vast expanse of the hall and when I called out I was answered only by a jarring echo. I imagined there must be a bell-pull somewhere to summon someone and looked around for a rope or sash. No such thing was to be found. Should I start going through the other doors leading off the hall in order to find out what was occurring here? The whole thing was becoming absurd. I had visions of blundering into a boudoir and encountering an initially startled, then outraged, Lady Degabaston, and thereby foregoing any chance of obtaining employment as a result. I would be guilty, in her eyes, of a total lack of patience and decorum. She might even think I was taking the opportunity to try and lay my hands on the family silver.

Wandering around the hall with my cane, as loudly as I could whilst trying to make up my mind what to do next, I spotted a huge pendulum-driven grandfather clock secreted in a carved ornamental niche in one of the far corners beneath the imposing staircase, and so I closely examined it. But that too, like my own timepiece, had stopped working. The pendulum nestled sharply to the left in its glass-fronted column niche, and the clock-face showed a perpetual hour of twelve precisely.

Confronting such "Alice in Wonderland" nonsense as this was not pleasantly diverting; it was highly frustrating—in real life.

Perhaps I should seat myself in the hall and wait for someone else to pass through it while they were going about their usual business. Or perhaps I should go outside and try and find the stables the servant had mentioned in case he was still there. Again, would I be breaching etiquette? I decided on the former option, sat down on a chair from which I could keep most of the hall under observation during my vigil, rested my cane across my knees, and carried on waiting.

Another hour must have passed, though my watch was still useless to confirm it.

Finally the bony myrmidon reappeared. He was making his way down the staircase, an expression of indifference on his curiously malformed and wizened face. I got to my feet and stamped my cane on the tiled floor, my sense of frustration having well and truly boiled over.

"Look here," I said, "what do you mean by keeping me waiting all this time without even a word of explanation?"

In a nonchalant fashion he crept close to me, then—menacingly—closer still, and bent his head forward as if confiding in me with a secret; his distorted face was only a few inches away from mine. I wanted to draw back, for his breath had a rank, sickly odour to it, like rot, but instead stood my ground as he spoke, suddenly becoming loquacious.

"Lady Degabaston has asked me to convey her apologies to you, sir," he said.

"Is she going to interview me or not?" I replied.

"Lady Degabaston requested a room be made available for you, sir."

"You haven't answered my question."

"I am not in a position to do so, sir."

"A room you said? What, to stay here overnight?"

"Quite so, sir. Where else would you go?"

"I have no change of clothes. No luggage."

"That has already been taken into account, sir."

"And the interview will definitely be tomorrow? Has her Ladyship been taken ill or something?"

"It is an old agony, it is the daylight. Shall I show you the way up, sir?"

Now he was simply babbling. I hesitated. Perhaps this was a definite sign the interview was a mere formality. She could hardly put up one interviewee after another at the abbey, night after night. Perhaps she knew how desperately I needed paid work. But still, she was rather taking me for granted and, after all, I had my sense of pride. I bristled at being treated in such a cavalier fashion.

"This is rather inconvenient for me."

"Really? Follow me, sir."

The servant withdrew from close proximity, turned around, and impatiently beckoned at me to accompany him as he sauntered back up the staircase. He did so in an offensive, offhand manner, as if directing me round to the tradesman's entrance. My sense of pride bristled again—though this time I kept silent.

He quickened his own step the instant I myself began awkwardly to climb up the stairs behind him, almost dancing to the landing above, despite his great age, so that he could look down and coolly observe my own laborious ascent. Was he actually trading on my sense of pride?

There was a maze of vaulted passages leading off from the landing, and we navigated two or three turns before entering an antechamber festooned with framed sketches and even a couple of landscape paintings. All were depictions of Thool Abbey and of its immediate environs, bathed in moonlight. They were by the same hand, I was sure, and, although I could not identify the artist concerned, they had a garish lack of craftsmanship which indicated they were the work of an amateur enthusiast within the family, rather than that of a dispassionate professional from outside it.

We next passed down a long, panelled corridor, up another short flight of steps into a farther corridor; one which seemed vaguely to narrow and shrink as we went along it and which abruptly terminated at a slightly crooked door. A dark wooden supporting beam in the wall, also slightly askew, jutted out at the top of this portal. The servant pushed open the door, stood to one side, and ushered me towards the interior. Once I was over the threshold I began to take in my surroundings.

"I will leave you to make yourself at home, sir," he said as he closed the door from the outside and again departed.

I went to the window and noticed the shadow of the projecting edge of the roof above, blocking out a strip of the late afternoon sky. A woodland, mostly of convoluted trees, pressed up close to the patch of lawn directly beneath me and stretched across into the middle distance. With some effort I managed to get one of the latticed window-panes open and, looking directly downwards, saw timber-framed supports, grey with age, lining the structure.

This room, then, was hidden away in a space under one of the eaves of the roof in a Jacobean annexe that had been—somewhat incongruously—tacked onto the rear of the mediaeval abbey. The angle of the slope from the ceiling to both sides of the oriel window was acute. Nevertheless, into this oddly shaped room had been crammed a narrow double-doored wardrobe with an interior mirror on one of the doors, a small writing desk and high-backed green leather upholstered chair, a small empty bookcase, a trunk, and a sleeping-bunk recess of the nautical type. The furniture was antique, of sturdy chestnut wood, though not well maintained. The bed linen was musty and had the faint suggestion of mould. In the wardrobe (which I had expected to be empty) there was a row of jackets and trousers, mostly tweeds for the country, but additionally a lounge suit and formal evening wear. Resting at the bottom there was also a portmanteau, which I found to contain a gentleman's travelling kit, some relatively clean shirts, and assorted toiletries including a safety razor, toothbrush, brushes, boot polish, and soap. I saw a small handwritten note pinned to the other, non-mirrored, door in the wardrobe declaring:

*Traveller, avail yourself of these contents freely during your stay.*

Most curious of all was that when I tried on items of the apparel I found they fitted me very well indeed. Had I myself chosen them off the peg I could not have selected a better fit. True, the cut and style were some twenty or thirty years out of date, but there was nothing about them so unusual as to make them particularly noticeable in the 1940s; particularly in the countryside, where garments are favoured for their durability, not for being fashionably up-to-date. All in all the suits and sundries (including the two pairs of shoes and a pair of walking boots) were of a much superior quality to any I myself owned; including the "Sunday Best" suit which I was now wearing. To remain at the abbey then, even at such short notice, would not present an immediate problem.

My fob-watch still refused to work, however. I would ask the servant at some point if he could provide a clock.

Hours passed, but still the servant had not returned. I could mark the passage of time only by the sun gradually dipping towards the horizon through my west-facing window. It appeared I had been forgotten once again. I wondered whether I would be called down for dinner or if a repast would be brought up to me in my room. The fact that I had scarcely touched the meal that had been laid out for me when I was in the library now seemed a mistake on my part. That may have been the only food I would be offered all day. The imposition of rationing in aid of the war effort had worked to regulate most appetites, though mine had never been great to begin with: a man who is already half-crippled learns it is prudent not to gain excess weight.

I lay for a while on the bunk with its musty sheets, turning my thoughts over and over, and eventually found myself dozing, drifting in and out of consciousness as the shadows lengthened in the room. There was nothing else to do.

When, finally, I awoke fully it was dark, though how long it was since the sun had set I did not know. My first thought was to locate some candles, but then, immediately afterwards, I thought of the blackout regulations. All parts of the country were subject to them, even in this remote spot where officious A.R.P. wardens were doubtless few and far between. I made my away over to the latticed panes of the projecting oriel window, which alone stood out in dim relief within the room, even though the evening was a moonless one. By fumbling around the window edges I located the interior wooden shutters but did not close them. First I had to find those candles.

My vision had now adjusted sufficiently to see the outline of large objects in the room, and I homed in on the trunk situated in the far corner. It proved, luckily, not to be locked. There were various objects inside which I could discern only by touch, and my fingers finally passed across a couple of waxen cylinders beside which lay a small box with a sandpaper edge whose contents rattled when shaken. I was in luck. I lit one of the matches and then one of the candles. I was surprised to discover the thing was jet-black, and the smoke it gave off had a queasy, sickly odour that I could not place.

I set the candle down on the writing desk, fixing it with blobs of hot wax into the base of a conveniently dry inkwell, closed the oriel window shutters, and settled myself into the high-backed chair. Those shutters would satisfy any wandering A.R.P. warden. Night-time bombing raids by the Germans had been as common throughout this October as they had been during September, though it was said—back then—that the Luftwaffe had failed to achieve air supremacy over Britain due to our valiant island efforts. The enemy were certainly not going to run out of fuel for their bombing raids; their socialist friends the Russians were still providing more than enough of it to assist in Britain's obliteration from the air.

I began again to think of food and wondered whether I was likely to be summoned to dinner; whether I was not invited; or

whether I had slept through the hour at which it was normally
taken. My wondering was answered when I opened the door to
the corridor outside my room and found that a small supper,
not dinner, had already been provided for me. The same meagre fare I had scarcely touched at luncheon greeted my eyes. It
even looked to have been laid out on and in the same pieces of
crockery and fluted wine glass; moreover, what I had not consumed had not been taken away but simply added to with
more of the same!

Despite my disappointment, I did not make again the mistake I had made earlier. Hunger and thirst overcame lack of enthusiasm for what was on offer. The meal over, the laughable
repast inside me, I put the tray back outside the door. Was I
now to be ignored or merely forgotten until morning?

Sitting there, in the flickering candlelight, watching the
shadows lurch in the confines of the oddly shaped room, I listened keenly for the familiar noises that did not, could not,
come. I was a city-dweller, and my London had not slept
soundly for weeks; it murmured uneasily at night, waiting for
the next aerial blow against it to fall—cheated out of slumber
by the air-raid sirens; awaiting muffled booms, frantic whistles,
and pitiable screams and moans once the enemy onslaught exhausted itself for the night, and the "all-clear" finally sounded.
But here in the abbey; here lay the real countryside all around
me. I was miles from the nearest village, and my experience of
such a region was confined to books. I remembered reading of
the wind whispering through branches, nocturnal things shuffling through the undergrowth, their strange animal cries in the
darkness. I had not been informed that there could be a univer-
sal silence at night, abroad only in the wild places, a silence that
was so oppressive it seemed to close itself around one's beating
heart and threatened to stifle the pulse of life itself.

The food and wine I had taken did not revive me in the least. Indeed, I felt drowsy and exhausted shortly after having consumed them, so I prepared myself for sleep. I clumsily undressed, deposited my clothes in the wardrobe, blew out the candle, and then fumbled in the darkness to the bed-bunk. Slipping between the musty sheets, I laid my head on the thin pillow that had to be folded over in order to be remotely comfortable. Far too tired to continue thinking, my mind ceased wrestling with its own waking doubts and fears.

But the sleep that came was not dreamless, and now there marshalled in my brain a blackened host of nightmare imaginings, from which I could not so easily escape as before, since one of the central elements was the absolute conviction that to awaken before this dream had played itself out was to awaken into the dream of a lunatic-other who waited outside, ready and eager to take possession of both my body and my soul.

The nightmare began with a series of exhumations in an ancient cemetery. Ground-mist swirled through tottering headstones and tombs over which wreathed tendrils and vines riddled with a grey disease. The entire deathly scene was bathed in the sickly yellow light of a waxing crescent moon. This charnel place was situated in a remote hollow, and I knew that I, like those few others with whom I dared venture into the region, feared and shunned it as the haunt and breeding-ground of a nest of unclean spirits. We were all dressed in the Puritan garb of the seventeenth century, and our task was to locate the witch-corpse that had been buried with the ungodly book that stole souls.

For the whole of that night we laboured at our ghastly efforts, exhuming coffin after sloshing coffin from the depths of the earth, hauling them to the side of graves that rapidly filled

up with ground-mist. What we found inside those coffins confirmed us in our fear that monstrosity was abroad in the land;
none of the bodies had decayed, none made ready for the Day
of Resurrection, but were instead bloated flesh without bones,
their facial features distorted, their crimson-webbed eyes bulging from the sockets, with new blood oozing freely from all
their orifices, nesting within their caskets in a pool of their own
filth and gore.

We prayed for fortitude as we worked on, and we had fast-
ed until nightfall beforehand, but, one by one, our numbers
diminished as the terrors increased. The men quietly slipped
away, sickened to their very cores at what they saw, breaking
their solemn vows to persevere in the task.

Some of the things showed signs of movement after death,
some moaned obscenely, and some even murmured blasphemies against life itself.

But at last, after long hours of such hideous trials, the body
of the faceless witch-corpse, the very nexus of evil, was brought
up. There, clutched over its bosom in its puffy fingers, was the
ungodly book which, it was said, stole souls when read, yet af-
forded an infernal longevity even the grim reaper could not finally gainsay.

When I—now the last one left to complete the appointed
task—wrenched the vellum tome away from the witch-corpse's
grasp and turned its venomous pages in the light of that sickly,
dying moon I saw my own name amidst all the other familiar
names written in blood therein, and it had been added in my
own hand.

The nightmare was still vivid in my brain even as I awoke; and I
awoke into blackness. I felt I had slept for hours, and when I
stumbled across the unfamiliar room and opened the shutters I

expected to see daylight. But the outside world was as pitch-dark as it was within the room. Had the Germans, then, deployed some weapon against us that could block out the rays of the sun completely? I groped around like a blind man for the candle and the box of matches resting upon the writing desk. My eyes smarted at the sudden illumination from the match. I lit the candle's taper and then began to dress myself in items of clothing from the wardrobe. My bladder and bowels were protesting at not having been relieved and I knew that they, at least, could not be mistaken; this was morning and not still the middle of the night. There was nothing else to do except take the candle with me and go in search of a privy. Down the short flight of steps at the end of the narrow corridor there was an unlocked door, and I entered into a small, viridescent-tiled water-closet. I fixed the candle to the sink and relieved myself. Washing my hands afterwards, I saw that my face in the mirror above the sink looked remarkably haggard, as if I were suddenly in the grip of some illness. Crow's-feet I had not noticed before radiated from the corners of my eyes, even beyond the lenses of my oval eyeglasses.

The matter of this omnipresent darkness crowded out every other consideration, however, and I resolved to find someone who could provide an answer to the conundrum. Wandering along the corridors with the candle in one hand and my cane in the other, I called out periodically for assistance, but received no reply, until at last I found myself back in the great hall. There, other candles had been freshly lit, which at least indicated I had not been completely left by myself in the black vastness of this eternal night.

I heard a rheumy cough coming from behind the door to the library, turned, saw it was ajar, and then heard, further, a rustling motion. I called out but there was no response, and so

I entered, but not closing the door fully behind me.

Inside, seated at the central table and poring over a volume from the shelves, was a woman in a voluminous black dress of antique design, and veiled with a lace mantilla of the same colour. Though I could not see her face clearly, I saw her withered, claw-like hand, dotted with liver-spots, which moved on the open page of the tome in front of her. She was hunched over it, tracing the lines of text with a bony index finger.

"Excuse me," I said, after clearing my throat. "I need your assistance, madam."

Could this apparition actually be Lady Degabaston herself?

The thing raised its head slightly, turned in my direction, and a croaking voice issued forth from beneath the veil.

"Tell me, do you like these books as I do?"

Surely this could not be her; for if it was, had Lady Degabaston lost her mind? Had that letter of hers that I'd received been a brief interval of sanity in some lunacy of long-standing duration?

I attempted to humour her.

"Of course," I said. "But what time is it?"

"The time of privation, as well you know."

"What has blocked out the daylight? Is it the work of Germany?"

"What has nation to do with it?"

"The war, madam. Don't you even know France has fallen?"

"There is, and has always been, only one war."

Perhaps the befuddled crone had lost her reason during the Great War and never emerged from the horrors of that conflict, and her living here, practically all alone, except for the deluded servants, without any other outside influences, meant she had lost touch entirely with reality after 1914. But surely there must have been quite recent attempts by His Majesty's Government to requisition Thool Abbey and its estate; after all, a large number of other stately homes and large country houses were apparently required for the current war effort, not least as barracks or hospitals.

"Are you . . ." I began.

"Quit me now," she said dismissively, her gaze turning back to the page of the book beneath her hand.

The servant stood outside the library door.

"Breakfast for guests is served in the refectory, sir," he said.

I tried to question the wizened servant too, as he led me away, but he was wholly evasive and unforthcoming. As far as he was concerned it was now broad daylight, and my repeated insistence it was not so made him smirk contemptuously as if it were I who had suddenly taken leave of my senses. Nor would he provide a satisfactory answer when I asked him whether the old woman I had seen in the library was Lady Degabaston.

"I cannot say," he said. "I did not see her. And you yourself said she wore a veil, sir."

I ate alone, at a bench lit by candlelight, in the vaulted tunnel-like confines of the refectory. The breakfast provided was of the foulest: it consisted of some half-burnt mixture of cabbage, potato, onion, and sliced red meat. I forced it down, aware I would need sustenance for the journey ahead. I had to clear out of this madhouse at once.

When the servant returned to clear away my plate I said to him:

"Give my apologies to Lady Degabaston."

"Sir?"

"I have decided not to take up the position offered and am leaving at once."

"No transportation is available, sir. The horse is now dead.

We have no telephone."

"I'll walk to the station, then."

He smirked that offensive smirk of his while glancing down at my walking cane.

"Look out of that window," I said. "Do you insist it's the daytime?"

He gazed absently at the arched, black aperture.

"Sir?"

"Why the burning candles on the table, then?"

"Thool Abbey always gets rather gloomy. Will that be all, sir?"

Once I had changed out of my adopted clothes and back into the ones in which I had arrived, I made my way downstairs—with another candle to guide me—into the great hall. There was no sign of anyone lurking about, but I soon found the main door was firmly locked and bolted shut. It was necessary for me to scout around until I finally discovered a window which was not of too lofty a height along one of the ground-floor corridors. Placing a chair beneath it, I clambered up, opened the catch on the lead-latticed panes, and hauled myself over the sill to the outside. It was scarcely much of a drop to the soil at all, but I still managed to drop heavily. Luck was with me, though, for even with one stiff leg I did not turn an ankle. Quite how I would get my bearings in the darkness afterwards, I did not know, but I trusted in a plan to follow the wall of the abbey around its perimeter until I came to the carriage driveway. From there it would be a case of keeping to that track faithfully until I was finally free of the abbey altogether. I had a cane; I could walk sightless, tapping the path ahead of me, albeit with my limp inevitably slowing me down. It would be a gruelling trek, but anything was better than remaining at the abbey.

# Chapter Three

Through me did he become idolatrous; and through me it was, by languishing desires, that he worshipped the worm and prayed to the wormy grave. Holy was the grave to him; lovely was its darkness; saintly its corruption.—THOMAS DE QUINCEY, *Suspiria de Profundis* (1845)

It was torturous holding fast to my purpose as I crept forwards, footstep after hesitant footstep, through a dead-black landscape. I had the horrible sensation the void itself was pressing in on me, my vision having retreated into the blackened cellars of my brain. The only sounds that accompanied me on this trek were those of my own breathing and the crunch of flinty gravel shifting with each footfall—although the latter, at least, provided reassurance I had not yet gone astray. Gently waving my cane in front of me in a narrow arc also assisted me in keeping to the path, forestalling any entanglement with the clutching weeds of the overgrown lawn.

To walk in total darkness for any prolonged length of time is to invite disorientation and confusion. I felt certain I was proceeding always in the same fixed direction away from the abbey, but could not shake off the impression that the length of the driveway was fantastically greater than I remembered it. I told myself again and again it was only the restricted nature of my advance which gave rise to this delusion. But still, were the path to deviate even slightly over such a prolonged distance, it was entirely feasible I would not notice its gradually turning around on itself, and—after many hours of useless walking—its finally leading me back towards the abbey.

I became increasingly tired and footsore. The laboured incremental advance was taking an ever greater toll on my nerves. I longed for some break in the jet-black clouds I reasoned must be low overhead; it would be a relief just to see a handful of stars, some fixed point of reference. By such a sight I could confirm I was not trapped in a gigantic, Stygian maze.

My mind was playing other tricks upon me, too. I kept looking over my shoulder, even though I knew I would see nothing behind me. I could not shake off the idea something was following after, purposefully measuring its pace and keeping its distance so that I would be unable to confirm it was there by sound alone.

Nevertheless, I persisted in following the track, trying not to glance back instinctively, half stumbling with exhaustion, until at last the noise of gravel underfoot died away. To my immense relief I realised I must have reached the twin stone pillars of the stone gargoyle-guarded entrance. Tapping around with my cane in the trellis-work of the gates, which I found had been left open, I carefully slipped between them and stepped outside the abbey grounds.

As I did so I was swallowed up by an all-encompassing brightness.

I experienced an immediate wave of sickening vertigo. It was as if the world around me had suddenly been lit up by a single lightning flash of unimaginable intensity; I felt myself hurtling towards the ground, and in the instant before I lost consciousness and was seized by darkness once more, I caught a momentary glimpse of the outer world's familiar sunlit fields and clear blue sky.

When my consciousness was restored (I do not know how much later) I found myself awakening back in the bunk of my cramped room in the abbey. I raised myself up onto my elbows and looked about me. Candlelight illuminated the oddly angled confines of my monk's cell, and I saw a stranger, clad in a fustian frock-coat, who leant over the desk in front of the oriel window. He unclasped a large black medical bag and then rummaged inside it.

Becoming aware of my revival, he paused, turned, and addressed me in a curiously hollow tone:

"Please don't exert yourself, Mr Prior," he said, "let alone try to rise. You've been the victim of your own impetuosity."

He drew closer to me, and I judged his age as being somewhere between seventy and eighty. The skin of his face was a network of scar-tissue, while his whiskers and what sparse hair there was left on the crown of his head were both white as alabaster. His movements were stiff, even arthritic, as if he struggled with muscles not wholly capable of carrying out the orders from his brain. Despite this infirmity, his aspect was noble and patrician. When he leaned directly over me and his fingers fumbled for my pulse, I saw close-at-hand a nest of unseemly white hairs sprouting from his nostrils and ears. His breath was of the foulest; reeking like rot, like that of the bony myrmidon. So, too, did he possess that same asymmetry of the facial features, though his own hooded, bloodshot eyes were sunk even deeper into their sockets. His were eyes one would not care to gaze upon; for there also lurked the suggestion of an inner, deeper, *essence* of horror buried within them.

"Who are you?" I said, as he pressed me firmly back into the bunk until my head rested on a musty pillow.

"Lady Degabaston's physician. You may address me as Dr Cressop.'"

"Do you know what's going on?" I said.

"You were followed when you attempted to quit the abbey," he said. "What transpired thereafter when you crossed the border—I mean your collapse—was inevitable. You were then brought back for treatment."

"About the darkness . . ."

"Perennial night," he interjected, "is something you will, in good time, remember to adore."

Though his way of wording it was bizarre, it was the first admission from another person that I was not losing my reason and that the abbey was, somehow, wreathed in eternal darkness.

He lifted himself away from the bunk, crossed the room with a stiff-backed gait, and returned to his medical bag wherein he again began to rummage. Eventually he drew out a small bottle and a phial and returned, reseating himself beside me on the bunk. He poured a measure of amber fluid from the bottle to the phial. I could not make out the label on the bottle; its lettering was incoherent to me, though I thought I could discern a skull-and-crossbones symbol.

"What's that?" I said.

"Swallow," he replied, holding out the phial to me. "It will assist your recovery."

"Poison? I don't think so."

Something akin to a sneer crossed his features and, to my surprise, he lifted the phial to his lips and swallowed the draught in a single gulp. Then he refilled the container and held it out to me again.

"Drink it at once or I will force it down your throat."

I did as I was told. It was bitter to the taste and left a cloying residue on the tongue. Dr Cressop withdrew a short distance and turned the chair next to the desk around, seating himself in it so he could further observe me.

Gradually I felt an enveloping warmth radiate through my limbs, with my stomach the centre of its source. A cosy numbness took hold of my thoughts, smothering all the fears and apprehensions which had tormented me up until then; for what did such mysteries matter? I ceased to think of omnipresent darkness and the cessation of time. I felt ineffably content just to lie there in that Jacobean room under the eaves, and even the terrible face of the doctor seemed softened by shadows and candlelight. All the strangeness that had occurred thus far, and over which I feared I had no control, was but a dream, my dream, one of my own making, and could not really harm me at all. I was at its core; without me it did not exist, and I could surely bend events to my will. If I wished to, I knew, I could easily rise from the bunk and even throw away my cane and walk out of the abbey; not into night but into reality. Only I chose not to do so. There was no need to follow such a drastic course of action: since there was nothing to be afraid of after all, why *should* I wish to leave? It was far more pleasant to lie back upon the bunk and meditate in this delightful fashion, far more sensible, far more peaceable.

The doctor rose to his feet and left me alone.

I dozed pleasantly, lost in reveries of my own. What wonders there were in that draught!

When he later returned it was in company of eleven other people, who included the mysterious woman in the veil and the bony servant who had first ferried me to Thool Abbey. Each one of the new persons appeared incredibly aged, some with crooked backs, some with blackened or missing teeth, some with rheumy eyes clouded by cataracts, some with limbs that dragged. Even the deepening shadows in the room caused by the now-guttering candles did not mask the full extent of their decrepitude. Bizarrely, some even wore antique apparel of a past era, complete with white periwigs and bearing powdered faces.

My dreams had taken yet another strange turn, but I was not in the least alarmed; rather I calmly regarded my visitors with no other feeling than that of appreciation at their benevolent concern for my welfare.

They crowded around the bunk, murmuring amongst themselves.

"He has taken the draught, I see."

"He sees and hears all, but cannot speak."

But in this matter one of them was wholly in error, I thought. I felt I could certainly speak, should I wish to do so. There was no need to settle the question by putting it to a vulgar test. It simply amused me not to speak; to take in this outré tableau silently as if I were really struck dumb.

"You were not yourself affected?"

"This form has grown accustomed to it," replied the doctor, "since the old agony of the life heretofore."

"There is much labour before him," said the woman in the veil.

"Aye, milady, there is."

"Make him fit and ready for the task then," she said.

At last I had confirmed the identity of Lady Degabaston, and I smiled at the thought I had been right in my earlier deduction. It had been senseless for them to try and keep the secret from me by mystification. Didn't they realise I had always been one step ahead of them? Didn't they realise this was *my* dream and that they were simply phantoms conjured up in *my* brain, owing their very existence to the power of *my* imagination?

But then the shades were upon me, holding me down. I resolved to cry out but a gag, some foul cloth rent from a winding sheet, was wrapped around my mouth. The faces pressed close to my own, the smell of rot on their breaths unbearable. They proceeded to tear open my shirt front, exposing my bare chest. All my equipoise was dispelled in an instant. This was not merely a dream and I was not simply its dreamer.

The doctor retrieved his medical bag while the others continued to hold me down, and their stares of triumph pierced me to the core. From the bag he took out a series of three large glass jars, each of which contained some writhing, hideously white organisms the size of a forefinger. As I struggled more frenziedly than before (though just as futilely) he unstopped one of the jars and withdrew the first of the creatures with a small pair of grubby metal tongs. The thing curled and twisted in the grasp of the implement, it being just as much of a prisoner as myself. I thought it to be a graveyard-worm, bleached by lack of exposure to sunlight, some monstrous albino that crawled towards freshly deposited coffins buried deep within the soil of the earth; but there were tiny suckers on the underside of its body, and through these it fed. As the doctor carefully placed it upon the flesh of my bare chest, it attached itself there gleefully, pulsing with renewed life as it began to draw my blood into itself. It turned from white to pink to crimson, its slimy skin translucent, and I looked down at the gorging leech as it increased in volume the longer it nestled on my chest.

The doctor repeated the process, drawing from the jars more of the loathsome things; until, finally, a multitude of such leeches were feeding upon my lifeblood. I watched with disgust as each, in its turn, changed colour from white to pink to crimson.

The spectral crowd gathered around me ceased to hold me down, for my struggles had become perfunctory; I was being drained and weakened by the loss of bodily fluids. As they removed their hands from my person, some began to mutter amongst themselves in a horrible species of vile self-satisfaction.

"The transmutations begin."

"The red vines of youth, enough for all."

"Ah, suppleness returns to my limbs."

"The dance of the scarlet ceremonies."

"Praise be to the Lord of Tophet."

"Through us did he become one."

"No more to dread the latter Lammas."

"Generous is darkness, great its bounty."

My head swam and my vision began to blur. I thought I saw the left eyes of the denizens pulsing obscenely, now entirely blood-red and bloated.

"We must cease, for the youth is almost drained," said the physician.

There was a collective groan of disappointment and the small, gruesome crowd began to drift away, withdrawing to the hidden chambers deep in the abbey whence it had issued in order to attend this obscene feast. Likewise, the doctor carefully began to dislodge the gore-bloated leeches from my pale flesh, returning them to their glass jars, wherein they now wriggled and curled in sated delight.

He raised my head upright, forced down my throat draught after draught of the amber fluid, and then, like the other denizens, he too drifted away; finally leaving me alone, drugged and utterly exhausted.

I must eventually have fallen asleep after that terrifying experience. The drug—mercifully—had kept further dreams at bay, for which boon I was grateful, and when I awoke again some measure of strength returned to my limbs. I rolled out of the bunk, setting myself upright on my feet, and instantly became aware of an overwhelming thirst. My tongue felt dry: my throat like furnace-baked clay. Someone had left a pewter jug upon the desk, with a handwritten note beside it; I glanced over the latter very briefly, but was far more concerned with assuaging the dehydration which seemed to have shrivelled up all my viscera. Though the water was warm, brackish, and bitter, I drank copiously, directly from the jug, until it was drained to the bottom. Feeling light-headed but no longer ravaged by thirst, I took up the handwritten note and read it—more attentively this time—by the light of a half-consumed candle that must also have been placed on the desk by the person who had brought up the jug. The note ran as follows:

> *Now that you have partaken in the initiation rites required for permanent residence in Thool Abbey, it is incumbent upon you to begin the outward work for which you were chosen; viz., the cataloguing of the contents of the library. It is solely by this method, as we have discovered through long experience, that any approach to the central book can be realised. You may harbour foolish doubts concerning all this, but it is our duty and obligation to warn you that failure to comply with the terms of this pact will result in the gravest of penalties. Your signature, when appended below, will signify your solemn, irrevocable acceptance of our dominion in this regard.*
>
> *[illegible signature]*
> *[X] ...............................*

This farrago of nonsense-ravings left me completely unmoved. It only strengthened my desire to get out of this prison of an abbey as quickly as I could possibly do so. I was being held captive, being drugged and tortured; naturally my mind would display definite signs of giving way under such horror. It was as if some outpost of a deranged, home-grown Gestapo had buried itself in the heart of the English countryside.

I even considered the idea I had been gassed with an enemy nerve-weapon and, at this very moment, was locked up in an out-of-town asylum; locked up in isolation alongside other victims who had been driven insane.

But such wild speculations are those of a paranoiac.

Once more, bodily escape was the only recourse.

This time, I thought, I would take a different route. I would avoid the driveway altogether so as not to be snared again in the same dark perils as before. I would make for the woodlands at the back of the abbey, the same region I could see now, in lunar light, through the oriel window. That strangely huge moon must have risen while I was drugged, and its dark left half, pocked with crater-shadows, signalled it was in its waxing phase.

Knowing this attempt would involve clothes suitable for rougher terrain, I dressed myself in sturdy country apparel from the wardrobe. I substituted my cane for a stout walking stick which lay, partially concealed, at the rear of the wardrobe. I thought the find a happy omen, though it was with a pang I left my cane behind: the trusty thing had, over the course of years, become an essential part of my movements outdoors and this other aid would be unfamiliar to me. But I had to be practical.

Finally I took up the half-expended candle to guide me down through the passageways and stairs, and stepped outside my room.

The first part of my escape route was uninterrupted; the corridors were devoid of any denizens. Like the bloated leeches which had gorged themselves on my lifeblood, they probably rested after feasting, hour after hour, needing to digest their unholy nourishment slowly whilst hidden away from view and dispersed singly within the multitude of coal-black rooms within the abbey.

Rather than making for the great hall at the front of the structure, which route I knew, I took a sharp turning that led downwards via a narrow staircase sloping to its rear, a route within the confines of the mouldering Jacobean annexe. I made as little noise as possible, trying not to use the stick as I would my cane in case my clumsiness with it should give away my presence. When I reached the ground floor I came upon a short passageway; its ceiling curved like that of a tunnel-roof, the brickwork underfoot littered with ragged piles of yellowed newspaper dating from more than a century ago. At the end of the passage was a peaked wooden door, with a grille-window, and fastened by a simple latch. It was unlocked and opened inwards, though the hinges were caked with rust, and no small amount of effort was required until (protestingly, with the bottom edge rasping against the floor brickwork) I eventually managed to pull it open wide enough to slip myself through the resultant gap. I had feared the noise I made would be enough to call down a horde of pursuers upon me, but the tunnel-like nature of the passageway must have muffled the sound and saved me from being detected.

Now I was outside in the cold, still, night air, and it was merely a short distance from the rear of the abbey to the outer fringes of the woodlands. By the yellowish glare of the waxing moon, I could see clear across the sickly growth of untended lawn that separated me from the first of the endless multitude of gnarled trees. Even when inside those dense woods themselves, there would surely be enough light to guide me in safety; and one of the major disadvantages in my recent, failed attempt at flight would be overcome.

I advanced as boldly as I could, for a half-cripple, glancing back only once for a last look at the vast bulk of the abbey which loomed behind me.

I should not have done so.

Up there, in several of the windows of the Jacobean annexe, including the oriel window of my former room, I saw the wizened faces of the abbey denizens peering down at me, their already crooked features further twisted and tormented by the effect of lunar shadows. Then, as if guided by a collective telepathic impulse, each one suddenly quit their stations at the same instant, ceased their vigils, and—I could not doubt it was thus—made haste to apprehend me and bring me back to the abbey.

I loped forward with a redoubled effort, covering the distance to the line of the front rank of sinuous trunks that were less than fifty yards away. It was impossible for any pursuer to catch up to me before I gained the fringes of the woodland.

So it proved, and I gratefully stumbled forward into the depths. I was then able, immediately thereafter, to make myself a much more elusive quarry for their manhunt. But although it would be difficult for the pursuers from the abbey to track me amongst the shelter of closely packed trees, briars, bushes, and thick undergrowth, my own flight became difficult in the extreme. To traverse only a dozen yards deeper into the woodland was a matter of fierce concentration and care; I had to avoid tripping on exposed ground-roots, to avoid entanglements with myriads of thorny, spidery limbs, and to make as little noise as I could whilst still forcing myself onward.

After several minutes of such effort I found myself close to exhaustion. Doubtless the drug they had administered to me played a part, as did the cumulative effect of the nightmarish shock after shock to the system I had borne; and though those strains would have debilitated anyone, yet I had the nagging impression that they formed merely a partial explanation. I felt somehow *permanently* enervated, not through an outside force, but rather due to a decay in my own internal powers; the type of enervation that comes only with advancing age. Could a few days spent within the abbey correspond to a span of years spent in the outside world?

I slumped down against the trunk of a tree, resting my back on it, my ears keenly alert for the sound of any rustling movement close at hand, but I could detect no sign that the abbey denizens had followed and were on my trail. Perhaps they did not enter the woodlands for some reason, and I had inadvertently found the one immediate refuge from them and from their tortures.

My hands, I now saw, trembled as if afflicted by palsy, and my breathing came in laboured gasps and wheezes. My heart raced in my chest.

Unless I rested for a time, I would not be able to summon up the energy required to carry me deeper into the woodlands and towards ultimate safety.

Long minutes passed—or at least seemed to—while I remained where I was, slowly regaining my strength and composure. My gaze was drawn upwards even while I marvelled at the silence of the woodlands. At night one would expect the silence to be occasionally punctuated by the distant cry of a night-bird or the furtive ground-scrabbling of foxes, badgers, or rats. The woodlands appeared devoid of all animal life.

High up between the web of branches overhead the huge, yellowish half-moon had, like me, remained motionless. But, I thought, it had no right to do so. Indeed, as I thought back to the moment I had first glimpsed it from the oriel window of my room in the abbey (over an hour ago by my internal reckoning), that unnatural moon had been fixed in exactly the same narrow portion of the blackened, starless heavens. Its suspension must have been some type of optical illusion, but I could not account for it, except as further evidence of madness or some after-effect of my having been drugged.

And then, quite rapidly, a ground-mist worked its way across the mazy vegetation, creeping with tentacular life, smothering everything up to waist height in its chill embrace.

I got to my feet, trying to shake off the stiffness engendered in my limbs. I had to carry on, though it would be now be even more difficult—due to the thickness of the mist—to avoid any perilous roots or other such obstacles underfoot. I knew the direction to take and took my first, tentative steps forward when there came to my ears the distant sound of creatures howling, but drawing ever nearer. The noise came from ahead of me; heading *towards*—not away from—the abbey. How many there were in the pack it was impossible to tell, and it was the sound itself that caused me the greatest panic. What howled in the collective did not consist of dogs or wolves, for their throats do not make such unnatural sounds. It was as if beings of an entirely different order of existence from those of the natural world were playing at mimicry—though without the ability to carry off the deception.

The silence of the woodlands had been shattered. The region became a tumult of ominous, noisy motion, and timber-echoes of the howling din drew closer with each passing second.

I hesitated for only an instant, but in that same instant realised there was nothing for it but to retreat to the abbey and to do so as fast as possible. Either to press on in the hope of by-passing the danger and achieve final escape or to remain where I was and attempt to hide myself until the danger had passed, would surely result in my seizure by the unseen forces. Yet every fibre of my being, every instinct I possessed of self-preservation, told me to flee.

So I blindly turned tail, stumbling wildly back to the abbey whence I had come, heedless of the treacherous and obscured footing, almost catching my boots time and time again on exposed roots and fallen branches. But, through luck or some miracle, I did not lose my footing altogether and did not go down to my certain destruction.

Only once, in a small clearing, after I had blundered head-long into a bramble bush whose thorny, spindly limbs clutched tenaciously at the rough tweed of my clothes—and while I struggled to free myself by beating at the shrub with my walk-ing stick, tearing strips of fabric from my jacket and trousers in the struggle—did I dare cast a frantic glance over my shoulder.

The howling had ceased and was replaced by the sound of dozens of them snuffling at the earth, as if seeking for juicy, fat grubs underground. I believe they thought I was now firmly within their grasp and the chase had come to its end. Some thirty yards distant I could see only the humped backs of those teratological devils as the things circled aimlessly, breaking the undulating waves of the waist-high ground-mist, stark in the sickly yellow moonlight. The skin of those humped backs was as grey as stone, but here and there it was mottled with deep-red patches of lichen, like a cancerous blight, and from those patches sprouted needle-sharp bristles. The things were some parody of life—only in hell could they have been conceived. Mercifully, these abominations were not stood upright: they were perpetually doubled over, their heads obscured by the low mist. Inspired by their snuffling and by my own recent terrors, I wondered if they possessed long snouts, toothless at the front, their heads long and worm-like; all the better to fasten on hu-man prey and like those of the stone gargoyles at the gateway to the abbey.

It was that last, maddening conjecture which provided the additional impetus I required to escape the bramble bush. In-stead of seeking to disentangle myself, I instead forced a path directly through it, leaving behind strips of torn outer clothing, with abrasions and cuts on any exposed skin. Once I was on the other side, I gained the outer edge of the woodlands rapidly, though the howling had started up again as the chase re-commenced. As I approached the lawn, stifling the screams that bubbled up in my throat, the noise of pursuit behind me faded, as if the things were baffled at my actions and the range of their activities was strictly confined to the woodlands themselves.

When finally I broke through from the last of the trees and to the safety of the untended lawn, such was my state of delirious relief and nerve-wracked exhaustion that I scarcely uttered a word of protest as the arms of the dozen waiting abbey denizens bore me into their all-encompassing embrace.

# Chapter Four

I go on, therefore, to commend the work of Mr A—. Though not of a moral nature, one might say of his points of genius, like one of the twelve Caesars, *Ut puto, Deus fio.*—THOMAS DE QUINCEY, writing as "X.Y.Z." in the *London Magazine*

*"You will labour, curse you!"*

Those departing words of Dr Cressop rang in my ears as the door of the abbey library slammed shut. The denizens had eventually dragged me there after my second escape attempt, allowing only time for me to change my clothing and to bandage my wounds in the upper room, whilst the doctor had delivered a long lecture on my future obligations. They filed me downstairs, to the library, and proceeded to chain my lower limbs to the front legs of a heavy, antique chair in front of the candlelit central desk on which rested piles of dusty books, within easy reach, all of which, Cressop said, awaited my urgent attention. The chair itself had also been chained to loops in the flagstones of the floor and was immovable. He had bandied before me a countersigned copy—the signature apparently in my own hand—of their ridiculous, enigmatic covenant. I admit the signature was an impressive attempt at forgery, but since I had no recollection of having signed it (the very idea was repellent), I did not regard it as evidence of anything other than a further refinement of their continued torture-process.

They had provided paper and pen, in the form of a quill with an inkwell and a blank bibliography (whose three hundred pages were nevertheless marked by alphabetical subdivisions) into which, I was advised, I was to codify the volumes laid out for my daily perusal.

Hour after idle hour must have passed, but I did nothing except observe my surroundings, even though most of the long vaulted chamber was lost in flickering shadows. And so I watched instead the multitude of candles slowly burn downwards, waning towards extinction. Only the arched lattice windows, situated between the high columns of the mahogany bookcases, offered an alternative distraction. I tried desperately to think of a way to reach them and to break out, to renew my escape attempts again, but the chains that held me captive were unbreakable. Distant reflections from the candle flames, unearthly in the coloured-glass panes, seemed to dance in the outside darkness, and I thought of them as evil sprites who mocked my own captivity.

The far end of the long vaulted chamber was utterly cloaked in darkness, and occasionally I thought I heard the sound of muffled breathing emanating from it. I wondered if all the denizens had quit the library, or whether one of them had surreptitiously remained behind—hidden—yet still an invigilator, noting the manner in which I assiduously ignored the books laid out on the table in front of me.

The sound of laboured breathing eventually became louder and began to be suffused with a rasping and indistinct whisper, then gradually coalescing into whole, definite sentences. The words themselves were indistinct, but I did not believe them to be in English, nor Latin, nor any language I could recognise. And as the incantation went on (for that surely is what it was) my stubborn refusal to attend to my work began to engender in me serious psychological distress. I knew the only way to cause the chanting to cease was to begin examining the volumes that had been foreordained for my attention. If I did not—if I continued in my resistance—then the chant would drown out every other thought inside my head, leaving me unable to think coherently at all.

Still loath to submit, I nevertheless reached out my hand to the nearest volume (an octavo-sized publication), took it up, and opened its grey, damp, leather-bound covers—smearing my fingers with the filth which coated the crater-pocked surface. Then the chant abruptly ceased; but its fading echo reverberated through my skull, an echo that threatened always to roll on and on and on like an endless, gurgling river of blood.

Lady Degabaston slowly emerged from the shadows, her features apparently dappled by a veil of black lace, her body clad in an antiquated ballgown of the same hue. She glided by me without a word, or any other such gesture of acknowledgement—her deportment phantom-like—before quitting the chamber and leaving me entirely to myself.

I had endeavoured to carry out my task. It was impossible.

The very first book I had taken up, once Lady Degabaston had quit the library, had physically twisted itself in my grasp and then snapped shut like a sprung trap in my hands. I sat there staring dumbly at the unfamiliar title and author's name embossed into its spine: *Verse from the Lunar Fever* by Antoine Melchior. I had glimpsed on one of the pages a few lines of some curious doggerel-poem before the volume had closed itself:

> the amnesiac thoughts
> of dying brains
> repeated but forgotten
> as the Death's-Head blooms
> in Molock's Garden

Despite my best endeavours, I could not get the book open again, and it was as if the pages and boards had been miraculously, instantly, sealed together to form one solid mass of pulp. That passage of free verse I glimpsed briefly was, however, now fixed in my thoughts—like an abominable prayer—and it was all I could do to stop myself from whispering the lines to myself over and over.

I set the book aside, resolving to come back to it later. Rather than trying to account for the mystery of its seeming self-animation, I resolved to go through some of the other curious volumes piled up around me on the immense table.

The next volume I turned to, *The Decipherment of the 221 Gates,* did not credit its author, but said title was blazoned across the front of the quarto-sized volume in decayed, bluish-green, raised lettering. It was bound in cracked, off-white boards apparently made out of hardened wax. I set the item down on the table, opened it, and turned the first few brittle, age-browned pages until I came to a frontispiece. This proved to be a reproduction of a daguerreotype portrait dating, I supposed, from the middle of the nineteenth century. A name, "Eleazer Golmi," was handwritten beneath it—doubtless some later addition. The person in the portrait was in his fifties with receding grey hair slicked back in a widow's peak from a high forehead. The face was rigid with the enforced stillness required of the sitter by the lengthy exposure period necessitated by copper plates. His dark eyes glared out from the page, intensely spectral across the vast divide of time. One of them, the right, seemed considerably larger than the other, giving him a strange, almost lopsided facial appearance; but the daguerreotype had been printed, whether through oversight or deliberately, *in mirror-image.*

I reached for the quill, dipped it in the inkwell, opened the blank bibliography at the first page, and prepared to make an alphabetical entry, intending to catalogue all the item's essential bibliographic features.

Turning back to the book *The Decipherment of the 221 Gates,* I found it had closed itself and must have done so while my gaze was momentarily elsewhere. I reopened the volume easily enough, it not having sealed itself into an apparently single block (as had been the case with *Verse from the Lunar Fever*). But the moment my gaze wandered from it once more, just as I wrote down the title in the adjacent bibliography, the thing happened again: the book closed itself.

With my next attempt I put my left hand (with fingers outspread on the open pages) on the volume to prevent its closing while I continued writing the appropriate entry in the bibliography with my right hand. This time proximate pages of *The Decipherment of the 221 Gates* crumpled and folded themselves around my left hand, and such was the brittleness of the paper it seemed the book was in danger of destruction should I make further attempts to catalogue it.

So I made the best perfunctory entries I could for the two items.

It is not to be supposed this series of outlandish happenings did not startle, alarm, and even terrify me. But my enforced stay at Thool Abbey was beginning now to accustom me to all manner of horrible marvels that, if experienced in the outside world, would have driven a sane individual to question whether reality is genuinely circumscribed by strict rules governing what is and is not possible. *But here,* where event after event was a violation of physical law, the fantastical did not seem so much a suspension of that law, but rather a malefic reordering of existence. I thought of a novice who sits down to play chess and is told by his opponent, contrary to established precedent, that it is black who always has the first move, and that the loss of a king is no more significant than the capture of a lowly pawn: for only once all the opposing pieces are captured does the game conclude, with no time-limit, and neither draw nor stalemate is permissible. And so, as the board is cleared, as the pieces become fewer, does it begin to dawn upon the novice player that such a game has no point, save its own absurdity.

I took the next book from the pile. It was *The Cult of the Psychomantium* by Claude Deschamps, translated by A. Muswell. Bound in black leatherette boards, with embossed gilt lettering on the spine, there was embedded in the front cover a small round mirror; one now layered with grime and dust and casting no reflection. I made another initial entry in the bibliography and then moved the nearest candle closer to hand. Opening the book at random, my gaze fell upon the following passage:

> La Société des Âmes Mortes has affiliates across Europe and is no longer confined to France. Its tentacles extend across not only landmasses and seas but also vistas of time and dream. Most of what now laughingly passes for diabolism and necromancy, for example, is an excuse for thrill-seeking, a bourgeois reaction against moral revolution. Nevertheless, it is in the metaphysical act of negation; in the wilful privation of Being; in the despotism of the abyss—to do anything for nothing's sake—it is only then that genuine maleficence is born and the eternal dead can reach back to self-create their own suicides.

The pages of the book suddenly turned themselves over, one after the other, as if caught by a gust of wind, though I could detect no such draught within the chamber. I attempted to turn the pages back to the spot wherein I had noted the passage above; but as I did so, the book turned in my hands and closed itself, the mirror-decorated front presenting itself to my gaze.

Some irresistible compulsion to see my own face reflected in that mirror took hold of me and so, with the aid of a handkerchief moistened by spittle, I began to clean off the grime and dust that had accumulated upon its surface. The nearest candle snuffed itself out, and the others inside the library followed suit, leaving me in total darkness. And then the mirror began to take on a curious aspect; for there emanated from its depths a radiant silvery-white glow, and down there—staring up at me through the still half-smeared surface—my own bespectacled features manifested themselves. But there was a damnably ironic distortion in them; the skin was that of an aged person, a labyrinth of wrinkles and deep-etched furrows, the thinning hair bleached white, the cheeks sunken, the mouth almost toothless, and the piercing, cobalt-coloured eyes stared back with the intensity of one demonically possessed.

I turned away in disgust but when I looked again—for the glow had increased in its intensity and commanded a mesmeric power—I saw the spectre-face in the mirror now riddled with decay, the skin pockmarked with patches of red lichen; and maggots writhed there.

Horrified beyond measure, and yet unable to tear my gaze from the apparition, I ran my fingers over my face (yes, the reflection followed suit!) and my sense of touch told me that, whereas some degeneration had undoubtedly occurred—a startling ageing of troubling import—nevertheless the reflection in that cursed mirror was not stark reality; for my flesh was not rotting away. Or, at least, *not yet*. But why, I thought, in a sudden flash of realisation, was that mockery of my face *not* reversed; *not* a mirror-image, but self-correcting; casting a reflection that was the right way around?

And when the charnel thing in the mirror smiled, it smiled moments before I did, just before I felt my own features twisting into a simulacrum of that self-same sardonic grin, and it was only then I broke the spell, only then I balled a fist and smashed it down on the surface, shattering the glass, cutting my hand, and bloodying the black leatherette cover of *The Cult of the Psychomantium*.

At once all the candles flared into life again and I screamed to be released from the library, screamed until Dr Cressop shuffled into the chamber, being lulled into quiescence solely by the promise of the calming phial, whose contents were drawn from the bottle bearing the sign of the skull-and-crossbones.

Weeks must have passed, but I came no nearer to the central book mentioned in the covenant. No longer did Lady Degabaston lurk in the shadows, observing my labours, for I was surely fulfilling my side of the bargain to the full extent of my now-declining powers. When I awoke after sleeping I was brought to the library and laboured therein until, after continued long hours, exhaustion overcame me and I was finally returned to my room high in the Jacobean annexe. Up there waited a phial of the amber fluid and thus a merciful, dreamless sleep.

On several occasions I discovered the telltale signs of leeches having sucked upon my flesh while I slept. But I was not troubled by memories of having been molested, and blood must have been drained from my body whilst I was unconscious. Fatigue troubled me in the immediate aftermath of such an episode, though it was clear the intervals between feasting were staggered in order to allow for my partial recovery.

Still, it was impossible to gauge the exact passage of time; for night, as ever, reigned supreme. Candlelight was not the sole illumination, however, for I often saw the death's-head moonlight, yellow and ghastly and unchanging—evincing no phases at all now, no waxing or waning—as it filtered through casements in the corridors through which I passed to and fro from the upper room to the library.

My meagre meals were brought to me twice a day (or perhaps a night—for there was no way to tell): always the same insufficient, unpalatable fare, carried in on a tray by the bony servant and taken away by him a short time later, whether consumed or not. The once-blank book of bibliography I was gradually attempting to fill was just a few useless short entries: the names of authors (where available) and titles (again, where available), sometimes a date of publication (often not), but always a description of the outlandish workmanship involved— not merely outré binding or other strange physical details, but always a record of those occult manifestations, such as self-animation, which I had experienced for myself.

Then, over a period of several weeks (no, say rather over countless hours of waking consciousness), I tried to catalogue a newly deposited pile of hoary books—though they were undated—which proved to be volumes XXI to LVIII of Thomas Ariel's *Kruptos,* that *magnum opus* of the bizarre.

The name Thomas Ariel was not without a certain recondite renown, and even I myself had been struck by the legends attached to that mystic philosopher's life and work. He had been the object of several enquiries from a foreigner of no fixed address, one Wolfgang Martz (in hiding from Chancellor Hitler's regime), and who had written to the antiquarian booksellers where I had laboured as a cataloguer in a gaslit basement. This person had offered fantastic sums for any item connected with Ariel (particularly his rare 1824 pamphlet, *The Mysteries of Dreaming,* which was not known to be extant), although we had been unable to oblige our German client in his search. It seemed there had been a meticulously organised purge of Ariel's work by the "rationalists" during the nineteenth century.

And here, before me, were thirty-seven volumes of Ariel's *magnum opus* at my disposal!

To my surprise, these volumes of *Kruptos*—of all the tomes that had passed through my hands before having been replaced

on the shelves of the abbey library—freely allowed themselves
to be read. With hindsight, however, I think this anomaly was
due to the fact that the series was incomplete. Had I sight of
the initial volume, in which, I supposed, Ariel's first principles
had been expounded, then some foundation might have been
laid for much greater comprehension. As it was, one gained only hints of the nightmarish assent propositions that lurked in
the background; dizzying revelations connected with the origin
of language itself and thus with its use in attempting to convey
ultimate meaning. Centuries alone would not have been sufficient to fulfil Ariel's goal, nor even aeons, for solely in eternity
could the author succeed, when he plumbed the depths of both
the "I AM" and the "IT IS" and reconciled those philosophical
polarities. The individual volumes, chapter by chapter, blazed a
speculative—but strictly logical and coherent—trail farther and
farther into the vast reaches of an abyss that could only be
eternal in scope, and thus require a span of existence, allied
with a fierce concentration, beyond the utmost capacity of
most mortals. It was not that Ariel had stooped, like certain
modern continentals, to Hegelian or even Kantian obfuscation,
but rather that he had engaged in a veridical attempt to storm
the very root of existence; and then encountered, not an infinite regress, but an absolute mystery.

The outside world, even one so strange as to contain a
Thool Abbey, almost became an irrelevance to me. I scarcely
noticed the sequences of sleeping and waking; I lived only to
plunge further into the enigmas wrought on the page by
Thomas Ariel in these precious fragments of his titanic masterwork. The thought I was a prisoner; the thought I had lost
my mind; all the terror and near-starvation; the draining of my
lifeblood as I slept: such concerns were as naught when com-
pared to the stupendous vistas of the true reality—which lay

behind what passed for the commonplace reality—as they opened up across those thousands of pages.

It was when I had catalogued *Kruptos* LVII, after working through what volumes of the series were at my disposal, that those weeks of obsession spent deliberating over Ariel's metaphysics were terminated by Dr Cressop. He had entered the library just after I set volume LVII aside. The "bibliography" now contained detailed notes on my own interpretations of the thirty-seven volumes of Ariel's masterwork I had read up to then. Of course this was entirely contrary to the "bibliography's" original purpose, but I could do no other than abandon the futile project that had been imposed upon me. Cressop pulled up a chair and began to examine what I had written. I might have anticipated anger to be his first reaction to this radical deviation from my appointed task, but he appeared to be completely unperturbed.

"It is not unexpected to us that *Kruptos* should have so deeply engaged your attention," he said. "It has led astray dozens of scholars before you."

"There were certain *physical* obstacles to bibliographical delineation with the other items," I replied.

"So you struck out upon this new line of research?"

"Indeed. The conjectures in *Kruptos* transcend all previous concerns. It is irrelevant what becomes of me hereafter. You can no longer claim any hold over me. Though my body is in chains, my mind is now free."

How much further could I pass into the absolute mystery were Thool Abbey to contain further volumes of Ariel's work; volumes beyond even LVIII, which I had not yet read? For it was clear that volume LVII in the series had marked only the first staging post of many which lay ahead in the metaphysician's tireless exploration of a realm boundless in its supernal grandeur.

Cressop chuckled to himself. It was an offensive chuckle, of the type common when a person is in possession of certain facts; facts unknown to the other party but which will permanently place them at a disadvantage.

"You have consumed but a crumb of knowledge and think yourself replete with wisdom," he said. "*Kruptos* is not for the understanding of the living."

"Then there are other volumes from the series, kept here in the abbey?"

"It does not matter. There is no end to *Kruptos*."

"Then how . . ."

"Neither is there any *beginning* to *Kruptos*."

"That cannot be. Thomas Ariel actually existed, the records show his birth date, his flight to Europe from bigoted persecution, his—"

"*Kruptos* formulated him."

"A book creating its own author? What madness is this?"

"*Kruptos* is only one of its names, and Thomas Ariel only what it used for its final cause."

I thought of the obsession that had gripped me during the period since my first discovery of the thirty-seven volumes in the series; how nothing else seemed of comparable significance, even the mysteries of Thool Abbey; how I had lost myself utterly in fantastic speculations whilst I carefully went through the arguments in those volumes; and how I had turned aside from the work of bibliography to writing out my own interpretations of what I had gleaned from *Kruptos* in the notebook that lay open in front of me. My gaze roved over what I had written down there.

"I am not Thomas Ariel," I said.

Dr Cressop leant forward, turned the notebook around to face him, and flicked through the pages, merely glancing at the contents as he did so, but obviously taking them in at an instant. He chuckled again.

"No, indeed. You are no Thomas Ariel. Still, *Kruptos* contaminates the understanding of all those who have read even some small part of the immeasurable whole: it demands expression in a multitude of forms. Even a cursory glance at what you yourself have written here confirms me in my conclusion you have copied ideas, rendered verbatim—though done so by you unknowingly—which have their origin in certain minor addenda from volume fifty-eight. Yet you imagine them to be solely your own creation. All such limited interpretations of *Kruptos* are already contained within *Kruptos*."

This wordy expression of amused contempt at my personal insignificance left me utterly speechless.

After a pause, Dr Cressop spoke again.

"You have wasted too much of your energy on this subject. Even now Ariel lives on, no doubt; and *Kruptos* still works through him. One of our agents, George Louis Burgess, finally encountered Ariel in 1903, managed to purloin these thirty-seven volumes, and brought them back to us here. But of Burgess it is better not to speak. He went much further down the mental path you have recently trod. Put these speculations out of your mind. As your physician you must listen to my counsel. You are done, at present, with *Kruptos*. And now it is time for your rest."

# Chapter Five

One night in high summer, when I lay tossing and sleepless for want of opium,—I amused myself with composing the imaginary *Confessions of A Murderer;* which, I think, might be made a true German bit of horror, the subject being exquisitely diabolical; and, if I do not flatter myself, some few dozens of useless old women I could frighten out of their wits and this wicked world.—Yet do not mention this, if you please, to anybody: for if I begin to write imaginary Confessions, I shall seem to many as no better than a pseudo-confessor in my own too real confessions.—THOMAS DE QUINCEY, 24 October 1822

My phantasmagorical labours in the library continued as futilely as before, with each new volume presenting near-insurmountable challenges to my appointed task; these challenges arising from the intrinsic terror at the blasphemies I encountered. Titles alone would suffice to communicate to the reader the abnormal nature of my endeavours, and to document each item in further detail—to reveal their actual contents or delineate their unique physical abnormalities—would be to become complicit in the transmission of a species of textual disease that had surely contaminated all the books contained within the library of Thool Abbey. I can only hint, I dare do no more: there was nothing of the sane, the natural or the teleological about them. Each one was riddled with chaos, devilry, and abomination. Thus, I cannot permit myself to put down in writing even their titles, let alone the names of the accursed authors of those other tomes. I wish I had not done so with the initial items I have already delineated in this account, yet I plead that these, at least, were already known to the world. To reveal even the merest iota of intelligence regarding the others, the items suppressed, banned, and disavowed, is to invite possession *post mortem*. Telepathy is a contagion of the dead (witness spiritualism); and the living divulge such secrets only at dire peril to themselves. It would have been better for me to forget the other books entirely; better still never to have had them daily laid out before me by the bony myrmidon as a form of malefic torture. And I will set no one else upon their track. I will not have another soul blasted by infinite decadence on my conscience.

Finally, then, in the matter of my being a captive and forced to labour in the library, I resorted to pretence. When working I was mostly unobserved, so I simply fabricated false entries in the bibliography, making up information, filling those blank spaces that remained therein between my ramblings about *Kruptos*. I rendered all my fresh handwriting blotted, or else otherwise illegible, and did not handle the foul volumes whose covers were invariably half-consumed by detestable patches of deep-red lichen.

I thought of Dr Cressop's mention of former scholars having been led astray by Thomas Ariel's *magnum opus,* of leeches that suck upon the flesh, and then of those hunched teratological monsters who lurked outside, their howling faces veiled by the ground-mist of the woodlands . . .

The "completion" of the first volume of the bibliography was announced by me at one of those intervals wherein Dr Cressop entered the library for his own purposes. I had noted that, when doing so, he seemed intimately familiar with the layout of the contents of the stock; scarcely hesitating before shuffling over to the section in which was contained whatever volume he wished to take from the shelf and then to carry off elsewhere to

some other part of Thool Abbey which he haunted. Whether
he was engaged in private research I did not care to enquire,
and although he must have surely returned whichever book he
had removed to its original place in the library (for in aggregate
the total number he consulted must have run to dozens and
gaps in the shelves were not apparent), I never saw him actually do so.

I might have expected my statement to evince congratula-
tions from him, for it was partially he who formed the motive
force of my cataloguing labours, but he displayed a bland indifference to the news of my having filled up the first volume.
Moreover, as if to compound the lack of response, he showed
no interest in examining the "bibliography" itself. Perhaps my
unauthorised deviation into the study of *Kruptos* (and subsequent mental contamination of the bibliography by its insidi-
ous influence) had convinced him I was now useless for the
rôle to which I had been assigned by Lady Degabaston prior to
my arrival at the abbey.

"There is to be another visitor to the abbey within the next
few days," Dr Cressop said, sliding a candelabrum across the
table and seating himself beside me. The musty stench of his
physical decay was unbearable. The nearer, brighter candlelight made his scar-riddled and furrowed features stand out in
heightened relief than when glimpsed across shadowy depths.
He stretched out an arm and his claw-like hand rested upon
my "bibliography."

Who was this "visitor" he mentioned? It had been a long
time since I had entertained the idea of another attempt at
flight, but could this new arrival be my means of doing so? So
overwhelming had been my sense of hopelessness and drugged
lassitude that I had given little thought to the possibility any
chance for escape would arise again. The labyrinthine obstacles

to it were starkly apparent to me. The bony myrmidon had ceased even to chain me to my chair in the library; first testing me by leaving the links unchained and then finally removing them altogether. And, after all, no locked cell is more secure than that of a mind imprisoned by its own ennui.

"You should be glad," Cressop went on. "You will finally see the sun once more. Time will cease to be arrested, at least for the few hours required."

I could hardly bring myself to reply, for such was the whirl of rising hope it befuddled my thoughts. I sucked at my tongue, noticing the loss of two teeth on the right side of my upper jaw. I did not recall them having fallen out.

"Visitor?" I managed to say, "But who—?"

"Do not be alarmed, there is no question of your being replaced. You are making fair progress, and doubtless will continue to do so. It is simply an ecclesiastical matter."

Baffled by his reply, I said nothing further.

"And now," Cressop went on, "I shall relieve you of your bibliography and convey it directly to Lady Degabaston. I doubt she will examine the fruit of your labours immediately, since she is currently occupied making preparations for said visitor; but, in due course, doubtless there will be a reckoning of accounts and a just reward for all your efforts."

For the next few days—again I use "days" through force of habit, but by its use I mean only to indicate those intervals where sleep and waking are separated from one another—I was imprisoned in my attic room beneath the eaves of the Jacobean annexe. The yellowish moon remained fixed in the same position as ever, its light as feeble as before; nothing had changed. There was no sign of any cessation of endless night, and although I often looked out of the oriel window eagerly for the

first traces of approaching dawn above the tops of the woodland trees in the distance, of blessed sunlight returning, there
was no such indication, despite the promise Dr Cressop had
made. Yet the things in the woods howled almost continuously,
deep in their far-off dark recesses, as if scenting some new arrival in the vicinity of the abbey (which other promise, you remember, Dr Cressop had also made).

I had become even more of a prisoner than before, since
previously I had at least enjoyed a minor liberty during my
time spent both in the library and in walking back and forth
from that same chamber. Now I was locked away in the attic
room during all my waking hours.

Sufficient food and water for several days (albeit meagre ra-
tions) had been left in a tea chest that had been hauled into my
room on the first occasion of my being locked in. I dined directly from unlabelled canned goods, such as bully beef and
beans, dating back, I suspected, to the time of the last European war. The tea chest also contained a wooden keg filled with
water, whose contents I had to use for both drinking and washing. Shaving was currently out of the question. My generous
hostess, or her bony myrmidon, had furthermore seen fit to
supply a tin pail. I used it for my bodily defecations; emptying
the contents directly out of the window to the soil below. So,
too, did the copious tea chest contain a supply of candles, and
for these I was indeed grateful. I could not have borne endless
hours of a darkness that was relieved only by the feeblest of
yellow moonlight.

No visit did Dr Cressop make with that magic potion upon
which I had come to rely. No soothing artificial oblivion prefigured a dreamless sleep. Now reigned the hours of insomnia,
exhaustion, then ghastly unconsciousness, followed by the revival of the recurrent nightmare of the ancient cemetery in the

remote hollow; of the blood-filled coffins whose decayed occupants were bloated flesh without bones, their facial features grossly distorted and half-dissolved, their crimson eyes bulging from sockets dripping blood, and of that damnable central book clutched to the bosom of the faceless witch-corpse; the book wherein I had written down my own name.

And so, in my waking hours, to distract from hideous remembrance of that again-recurring dream, I learnt every detail of my attic room—my prison; no inch of it was unknown to me. By candlelight I examined it from top to bottom and surveyed minutely every corner, every nook, every cranny. It fixed itself upon my brain like an impression made in a wax tablet. You cannot conceive of the isolation an emptied waking mind, one denied any new sensation, one rendered devoid, suffers. It falls back upon its own resources and finds them (alas, all too rapidly!) depleted.

I tried to force the locked door several times, but it resisted my efforts. I hammered upon it with my fists over and over again, but there came no answer. I would slump down next to it, my ear pressed to the wooden panelling, and occasionally I would hear the faint comings and goings of the abbey denizens, their distant footfalls passing along corridors or descending staircases, their ghostly voices, the words indistinct, murmurs in low tones, whispers like the wheezing of a last breath, and the muffled wooden creaking of the Jacobean annexe as its ancient structure settled as uneasily as the bones of a dying, paralysed patient turned over in a hospital bed.

The return of the sun was an event as stupefying as it was sudden. I was aware, of course, that when time ceased to be suspended it might mean dawn had arrived whilst I was sleeping and I would be aware of the night ending only after I awoke.

On the other hand, since I had no means of knowing the exact hour of night at which time had been suspended, its passage could begin to run once more in its natural course for hours before daylight began—or for mere minutes beforehand.

But the transition was not gradual at all. I was already awake when it happened; crawling around the confines of the upper room in candlelit semi-darkness, and running my finger-tips along the wainscoting of the walls, seeking to memorise the multitude of subtle, mandala-like patterns in the grain of the antique wood. And then, as if a titanic searchlight were instantly trained on the abbey, there flashed a steadily brilliant sunshine.

My eyes smarted, the pupils contracting with a sharp retort of pain; such was the immediacy of the switch from dismal gloom to intense illumination. I closed my eyes, took off my spectacles, and covered them with my hands, gradually accustoming my vision to the stark vividness with which it now had to contend by peeping through gaps in my fingers.

Outside, seen through the oriel window, was an azure sky of Mediterranean splendour, and, with my eyes rapidly making the adjustment then from night-dark to sunlight, I replaced my spectacles, clambered upwards like a grub from the soil, and made my way over to the casement in order to take in more fully the marvel of the thing. I opened the central, mullioned pane and a swirl of summer fragrance—the scent of innumerable wildflowers blooming in the woodlands—was carried in on the warm zephyr, dispersing itself to each quarter of the musty confines of my chamber. I leant out of the window, swallowing draught after draught of the intoxicating perfume, felt sunlight on my skin again, and almost lost possession of my reasoning faculties at its intoxicating ecstasy.

But what a degradation it also revealed! When I was sated

beyond measure by the blessed illumination I turned back and there was laid bare behind me, in the stark brilliance of the same light, the full measure of the sordid squalor of that cramped, foul-smelling chamber, and of the degeneracy to which custom and despair had gradually rendered me insensible. I longed to get out of that prison cell more than ever and even shouted aloud from the casement, calling for assistance and release. To be locked inside now was doubly unbearable, and I calculated the danger to my person of climbing over the sill and plunging down bodily into the band of excrement-coated soil directly beneath the casement! But the distance to the ground was so great that a jump from such a height would surely risk permanent injury; perhaps, *at best,* rendering my remaining good leg as lame as the bad but, *at worst,* resulting in my breaking my neck.

And then I saw him: a bulky figure advancing towards the abbey, wrapped in the clerical black of a soutane, topped by a wide-brimmed round hat, traversing the lawn, until he finally stood almost directly below, gazing quizzically up at me with both his eyes perfectly, *mercifully,* of normal aspect.

A priest!

"Sir, I am seeking admittance to the abbey," he said. "But no one has answered my summons."

After I had shouted down instructions regarding how he might gain entry (viz., via the latched door in the Jacobean annexe) and then gave directions that he should wind his way up along the backstairs until he reached me in the upper room, the visitor was lost from my sight. He had promised to follow my instructions faithfully, but I was assailed by concern he might easily lose himself in the structure's internal labyrinth or else, even worse, that a trap had been laid for him by the abbey denizens—a trap in which I had now played an unwitting part in having sprung. His arrival was, after all, expected by the likes of Dr Cressop.

But eventually, my ear pressed to the door, I heard the noise of a heavy tread coming down the narrow passageway outside that led to my chamber. Perhaps with two persons it might be easier to force open; one applying his shoulder without and one pulling from within. I was about to make the suggestion when the door opened inwards after the rattle of a key in the lock and a turn of the handle.

"The key," said the visitor, holding the object up for my inspection, "was inserted on the outside."

In a pathetic gesture of welcome, I grasped his free hand and shook it gratefully with both of mine. I noticed the visitor recoiled initially at the contact, but relaxed somewhat when I finally released him from my grasp. He wore white kid-gloves, an incongruous affectation for which I could not account, save that he perhaps disliked to be touched.

"Sir, my name is Saul Prior and I am being kept prisoner here against my will," I said. "I believe this place to be a dangerous madhouse and it is imperative we both leave at once—at once, I implore you, and without any delay."

"Held against your will, you say? I had certainly not expected this turn of events. What of Lady Degabaston? She it was whose letter brought me to the abbey on business. I am the Reverend Alphonsus Winters."

He bowed in a courtly fashion and removed his black, broad-brimmed hat.

I limped across the room and stooped to retrieve my walking cane. I meant to put as great a distance between myself and the abbey as possible. Now that sunlight had returned and with the assistance of Winters, freedom was assuredly within sight.

Turning back, I noticed him staring around the room in disbelief (no doubt at its squalor and decrepitude), and he still harboured about him an air of caution or even suspicion—as if he were the butt of an elaborate jest or as if it might be that the abbey were indeed a madhouse, and I myself constituted its sole occupant.

In the fever of the moment the name he had given had passed me by, but I soon realised I had encountered it before. Surely the Revd. Alphonsus Winters had been one of those clients on the subscription list of the Hampstead Antiquarian Bookshop, and thus a regular receiver of the catalogues which I had compiled there. I racked my brains to try and recall more; stalling for time by pretending to rummage in the desk and drawers for certain papers I insisted must be located before we could quit the abbey together.

His features seemed familiar to me, now I had the opportunity to examine them at closer quarters: the milk-white skin of his smooth, fleshy face, the unruly black eyebrows, the thin lips, the hair (surely false) styled like an eighteenth-century periwig. Yes, I had seen those features before: they had stared out of a photographic reproduction of him set alongside a review in a prim church journal. A review damning as "an evil sewer of superstitious mediaevalism" one of his own scholarly books; its subject matter revenants, ghouls, vampires, and demons. Such was the ilk which stalked through the lurid pages of that nightmarish encyclopedia of hell on earth, a book which I had then been prompted to read for myself. *The Damnable Cult of Witchcraft!* Yes, now I knew that name—and not only in connection with my catalogue and the purchase of certain occult tomes—for he was notorious in society! The Revd. Alphonsus Winters, "Priest in Holy Orders," yet one rumoured defrocked, and dubbed by the press "The Connoisseur of Diabolism"!

But he had never seen my likeness, or my person, until this moment, so I had the advantage over him. When I mentioned my surname he evinced no sign of recognition; and why should he recall it? A lowly cataloguer (whose book-lists Winters had undoubtedly scoured for possible research material) leaves his work unsigned. Now I suspected why he had come here to Thool Abbey: it was surely to avail himself of the unparalleled library, to delve deep into the infernal mysteries harboured therein!

*Was, then, Winters already an outside agent of Lady Dega-baston and the rest of that ghoulish horde gathered around her?*

All these possibilities flashed across my mind, and the Revd. Winters appeared to notice the turmoil in my thoughts. I tried to keep my face mask-like, impassive, so that he might not suspect the reason for my hesitancy, but some giveaway-element must have crept into my expression—some furtive hint in the mouth or eyes—for he finally said:

"You were in a hurry to leave, I thought. Surely the papers you seek cannot be so important?"

A hurry to leave? I had to stifle a laugh. Of course I was in a hurry to leave! But I was in no hurry to put my trust in a fellow-traveller of the torturers of Thool Abbey!

And then the darkness immediately snuffed out the sunlight.

# Chapter Six

It must now be asked whether children can be born of the union of the witch and the incubus, and the general opinion of theologians and demonologists is that there have been and are such progeny. One undoubted case, known to me, was that of the young authoress of a single, suppressed book entitled *The Reunion and Others*. Certain of the tales therein display an unparalleled intimacy with the forbidden arts of necromancy and malefic possession: and only an early death curtailed an even more potentially terrifying sequel to her already abominable blasphemies.—REVD. ALPHONSUS WINTERS, *The Damnable Cult of Witchcraft*, 1938

My visitor was more startled than I was by the abrupt transition from light to darkness, and the Revd. Winters exclaimed that he thought he had suddenly been blinded. If he were acting a part in order to lead me astray, then he was a convincing actor indeed: his initial cry displayed genuine terror.

"You are not blinded," I said. "Remain quite still."

"Witchcraft, then!" he hissed. "There can be no doubt!"

While I fumbled around in the dark for a candle (my enforced familiarity with the chamber's layout assisting me in this regard) I heard him reciting a prayer over and over—one rendered in Latin. I recognised it as the Angelic Salutation.

Hearing his earnest entreaties to Our Lady, Mother of God, it was hard to credit the notion that the Revd. Winters was secretly himself one of the diabolists and thus a part of the conspiracy against me. And yet—*and yet*—is it not written that devils themselves will even quote from holy scripture to gain an advantage?

He was becoming more palpably agitated.

"Do not move," I said again. "We shall have some light here forthwith."

I located the candle and, thereafter, also the matches, then lit its wick, and finally turned to my companion.

The Revd. Winters's face was paler than ever in the light of that flickering glow; a sheen of sweat glistened on the forehead above those bushy eyebrows. I thought also, for the first time, that I detected white makeup—a lady's foundation powder, no doubt—dabbed upon his skin. His thin lips twisted into a smile of relief, but it was a forced expression, an act of the will, and I believe he did so thinking it would be to my benefit—to aid *my* composure!

"When I advised you I was being held prisoner here," I said, "I told the truth, but I have not laid all the facts before you. It is not mere madmen who keep me here, though God knows I wish it were only—"

He raised his hand and made the sign of the cross over me.

"I already suspected as much," he said, cutting off my own explanation, "and as for the doubt you harboured concerning me—I harboured a greater doubt about you. I confess I thought it possible you were a fiend yourself. Yes, the letter that brought me here was indeed from Lady Degabaston, but I had my own reasons for accepting her invitation, trap though it might be. I know this region to be a cursed blight. I am already fully cognisant of the historic and demonic infestation that reigns, with abominable effect, in Thool Abbey. It radiates tentacles of spiritual contagion across most of Europe. To purge this spiritual cesspit, to exorcise this abyss of evil: that is precisely why I am here. My studies—"

"Well, the old remedy of bell, book, and candle will not prevail in this instance, sir. I am absolutely certain of it," I replied, breaking into his own account in turn and stating the true facts.

The priest's face immediately lost its amiable expression of fatherliness and he frowned, with inquisitorial steel, as if preparing to defend orthodoxy against a heretical doctrine on the lips of an infidel who was being put to the question.

Then a series of distant howls rose up from depths of the woodlands outside, issuing in unison from the throats of those teratological freaks like a hellish, offstage chorus.

I swear, I almost laughed at the thing; for their timing was impeccable.

The Revd. Winters, however, apparently had no urge to laugh but rather turned to look over his shoulder in the direction of the cacophony beyond the oriel window. Then he fairly staggered towards the nearest chair and slumped down into it, visibly gasping for breath.

"I have seen and heard enough in my time so as not to doubt the truth; and read more of unseen—even greater terrors . . ." he wheezed.

This person, I thought, this person was the man the press dubbed "The Connoisseur of Diabolism"? This powdered, dusty, effete clerical scholar, fit only to chronicle the drunken excesses of a lukewarm "Hellfire Club" or the puerile, evil-eye antics of the "Witches of Warboys"? This blubbering, whining wreck: was *this* "The Connoisseur of Diabolism"?

How much longer before the denizens within the abbey took action? If Winters were lured here for a purpose, the first part of their plan was achieved, and perhaps even now they were marshalling their forces in order to fall upon us.

I made the priest assist me in forming a barricade of furniture against the door into the chamber, for he had no idea, as I did, that the monstrosities of the woodlands appeared limited in their operations to their own habitat. And, of course, concerning the ghoulish-dozen resident within the abbey—I mean Cressop and his ilk—he had, as yet, so I assumed, no inkling; he knew only of the existence of the abbey's mistress.

"You have told me that Lady Degabaston wrote to you," I said. "Do you have the letter about your person?"

Winters nodded and commenced a fumbling search through his pockets for the document. His attention was still partially distracted by the droning chorus from the woodlands—the howling which rolled across the endless night as if the darkness itself were singing a song of its own madness.

Finally he located the item, drew a single sheet from the envelope, and then passed it over to me, his hand not steady as he did so. His eyes flickered towards the oriel window. While I examined the letter by candlelight, I crossed the room and shut the casement, deadening at least somewhat the continuous, bestial noise originating in the depths of the woodlands. The letter read as follows:

> Thool Abbey
> Gallows Langley
> Hertfordshire

Your Reverence,

We acknowledge receipt of your letter of the 23rd inst.

Your name, of course, is not unknown to us and your request to examine certain volumes of family history et cetera contained in the abbey library is one to which we are pleased to confirm we can accede. We look forward to making you welcome on the day proposed.

We note that you lay particular stress on the necessity of a morning arrival and early evening departure. Let us hasten to assure you no offence is taken by us at the time constraints you imply are imposed upon you and which oblige you to make such a presumptuous request. However, such are the multitudinous diversions of the library, not to say the abbey itself, that we hope, once you *are* here, you might find yourself free to enjoy our hospitality for a longer period than envisaged.

Again, believe us when we say that the series of books which you have authored upon the subject of recondite folklore are particular sources of pleasurable diversion to us during the dull nights of our perennial seclusion.

Yours truly,

Lady Caroline Degabaston

"Reading between the lines, this letter seems to me to be an only partially veiled threat," I said. "What induced you to take such a terrible chance?"

The Revd. Winters stared back, his eyes unblinkingly defiant. I was pleased to have roused him to a state whereby he had shaken off (at least in some small measure!) the dictates of fear imposed upon him by our immediate, macabre situation.

"I have previously told you, but you have not listened: exorcism! But, sir, I could ask the same question of you. What brought you here?" he replied, his voice now high-pitched and shrill.

"My coming here was entirely the consequence of deception. I was lured without any foreknowledge of what might befall me. I am a book-cataloguer by trade and—"

"Then you now have some detailed knowledge of the contents of the abbey library?" he interjected, far too eagerly for my liking.

"The world would be safer if that library were burnt and razed to the ground. I will not speak further of it."

"Yet within the Vatican library," said he, "there exist books forbidden to neophytes not spiritually trained to resist an unholy contagion: such books are not burnt, but kept and listed in the *Index Librorum Infernalium*."

Had the priest suffered what I myself had suffered—the

endless days devoid of sunlight, the horrors of confinement in this abbey of nightmares, the curious physical tortures of Dr Cressop with his leeches, the infinite speculations of *Kruptos* and the soul-destroying reverse teleology of it and those other tomes—only then would he have had the authority to instruct me upon the essence of evil. His knowledge was all secondhand; either thoroughly bookish or else derived from souls unburdening themselves of commonplace sins in the privacy of the confessional.

"It would be of greater profit to us both, in view of the gravity of the situation, were you to tell me everything you already know about Lady Degabaston," I said.

"Very well. But first, tell me, have you encountered the name 'Lilith Blake' during your own researches?"

"I recall her only book being very much in demand by certain wealthy collectors but quite unobtainable due to extreme scarcity—it was a collection of weird stories—"

*"The Reunion and Others."*

"What connection has this with anything?" I asked.

"I believe a copy of this book is contained within the abbey library, and I also believe it to contain a certain personal inscription by the author of tremendous import."

"I have not seen the book in question. Again, what connection has all this with Thool Abbey?"

It was then that the Revd. Winters verbally provided me with the following lengthy account of a certain episode in which the all-encompassing influence of Lady Caroline Degabaston became gradually apparent.

It was in Highgate Village in 1913 that I encountered the thing which called itself Lilith Blake, and it had already been dead for seventeen years.

At that juncture I was a relatively young man, one who harboured no thought of entering holy orders and—I am ashamed to confess it—one who was also wont to dabble amidst the then-fashionable twilight world of spiritualism. I was resident in Hornsey at the time, having obtained a teaching post in a local school. At night many a séance in the region saw my participation and, though most of these gatherings proved to be only opportunities for varieties of imposture, fraud, and hoax, still there was one convocation in a Highgate parlour—dimly lit by a turned-down, greenish gas-jet—wherein four "sitters," myself amongst them, conspired unwittingly to summon up a dark force that had waited with malevolent patience for the right moment to make itself known as it dreamed undyingly in its nearby charnel lair. I think it was weakened at that period, and thus telepathy could not carry its thoughts very far. Both the séance's proximity to the old western part of the vast local cemetery wherein Blake was entombed and our ignorant act of open invitation proved key factors to "making contact" successfully.

Do not think there was a dramatic manifestation at that séance. There were no floating apparitions, no ghostly tentacles of ectoplasm, no table rapping. I was merely told by the others, curtly, that I had said certain things in a voice not my own; that I spoke in the cultivated voice of a young lady, but one who would not give her name. I laboured strongly under the impression the others thought me to be a faker and a charlatan. For my own part, I have no memory of what transpired while I was under the spell: the period of my initial "possession" was a total blank. But the others told me what was said by me was manifestly deranged and they cut me off for good thereafter. The dear departed, they advised me, are neither malevolent nor hostile but return only to impart messages of spiritual guidance and comfort.

And over the following nights certain recurring dreams took hold of me, dreams wherein I was wandering through a vast hillside necropolis, picking my way through endless monuments and tombstones; a low mist writhing across the undergrowth while above me shone the ghastly light of a yellow-tinged moon. That some final destination was intended I could not doubt, for I was being drawn against my will towards the centre of a hideous labyrinth.

Night after night the struggle went on and my health was badly affected by it. I felt dread at the prospect of sleep, and resorted to certain powders in order to ward off unconsciousness. When the supply of them was exhausted and my apothecary was obliged to send off for more of the same, there was a brief interlude between the doses, and it was during a night's sleep in said interlude that I made my closest approach to the heart of the hideous labyrinth itself; to that telepathic nexus which projected tendrils of thought in which to snare its chosen victim. By some circuitous pathway I had not trodden before in my dreams, I finally found myself within a circular cluster of sycamore trees, almost inaccessible due to the bramble bushes that flourished in the undergrowth leading up to it.

There was an immense tomb, its arched roof covered with sickly looking ivy, the corners adorned with elaborate finials, though much of the masonry appeared to be in the process of rotting away. It seemed centuries old, but its design belonged to the Gothic Revival style of architecture that had its recent heyday in the reign of the last queen upon the throne. Miniature porticos had been added to the square exterior of the structure, and on one side there was a

memorial tablet, of green marble, bearing the bleak epitaph:

LILITH BLAKE.
BORN 25 DECEMBER 1874.
DIED 1 NOVEMBER 1896.

At the front of the tomb, at the bottom of a short flight
of steps, there was a peaked trellis gateway, and beyond this
a deeper, longer flight of red-lichen-covered stairs that led
down directly into the underground vault wherein the
corpse itself was interred.

As I stood there, in that dream, gazing into the aperture, obscene visions rose up in my mind; visions of dead
bodies which did not rot, whose decay was slowed in the
early stages, and which were thereafter fixed in a state of
indefinite suspension once they were buried. Their exist-
ences were sustained by strength of will to dream, by morbid imaginations that constituted a pact with death, and
were further empowered in this unholy design by the arcana of a forbidden auto-necromancy.

Whatever dark force lurked down there desired me to
open the gate of its tomb, to descend those lichen-coated
stairs and go down into the inner crypt to join with it in a
monstrous subterranean eternity of hell.

And I knew then I stood upon the very threshold of my
own damnation.

The morning after, when I awoke, I found my wrist cut,
and upon the notepad by my bedside I had written down
certain foul instructions addressed to myself, *but instructions not in my own handwriting and yet which were written
in my own blood.*

I burnt the offending paper and resolved to have nothing more to do with such occult sciences as spiritualism. These hideous events I took as a warning to which I was obliged to take serious heed, and they led me, under grace, to reconciliation with the Holy Mother Church from whose nurturing influence I had strayed. By prayer, by fasting, by the sacraments, the terrors of the Highgate episode fell into abeyance. Eventually, no longer did I require even the chemical powders I had habitually used to ward off sleep; and so, over a period of further months, my dreams gradually became decontaminated of those malefic influences. My devotion to the Church only increased, a vocation for the priesthood was revealed to me, and in due course I entered the seminary of the Scots College in Rome.

The intervening years form no part of this account, but suffice it to say that a certain wonder at the unknown lingered on in me; perhaps inevitably, because wonder always lurks where there is the unknown. Mysticism, which is the greatest romance of all, informs a disquietude with earth and an aspiration for heaven.

Secure in the true Faith, I ventured upon study of the history and background to the spiritual contagion that had once almost snared me in its grasp.

And then I began to pen the scholarly books which have since made my name known to the reading public, but always with the purpose made clear therein that in delineating the multifarious masques worn by witchcraft, diabolism, and necromancy, in all their varied and terrifying forms, my prime motivation was to issue a warning to the modern reader of the infinite danger in this alternate reality, one spawned from darkness, not light—and whose evil handmaiden is atheism. Again, I say, my prime motivation was to warn of this terrifying alternate reality: one that offers the absolute certainty of eternal corruption.

And what has been my worldly reward? Jeers, scorn, laughter, and abuse from all sides! Incredulous scorn as a "boon" companion, mockery as a "fitting" tribute, and repeated denial from the Church of the *Nihil Obstat* and the *Imprimatur* for all my books when they were submitted for ecclesiastical approval.

Finally, upon the appearance of my latest volume, *The Damnable Cult of Witchcraft,* there came my suspension by the bishop from preaching, from hearing confessions, and also the further restriction of my office to saying only private Masses for the dead (this last condition, as was apparent to all, an irony of staggering proportion!).

But in mentioning these, my recent ecclesiastical travails, I have digressed too much and must return to my central topic.

It was during research for *The Damnable Cult of Witchcraft* that I happened across the name Lilith Blake once more, and this emerged in connection with the Degabaston family and its centuries of tenure at Thool Abbey. Just after the dissolution of the monasteries by the adulterer and tyrant Henry VIII in a campaign of mass plundering, Thool Abbey and the surrounding grounds thereof were acquired from the Crown by the nobles of the Degabaston line (whose arrival in England dates, as you may know, from the Norman Conquest). The first to dwell in the abbey itself, in 1539, after the expulsion and wilful persecution of the poor abbot and his monks, was the notorious Charles, Sixth Baron De Gabaston, born in 1509, favoured lackey of the Tudor anti-Papists. A rogue secretly contemptuous of all religion, and well versed in the worldly Machiavellian doctrine espoused in *The Prince,* he it was who rapidly rose to preeminence during the second half of the sixteenth century, consolidating his ill-gotten gains even as the very Crown of England itself was skilfully reduced, in turn, to the miserable status of an insufficiently salaried puppet of the same godless plutocrats who wielded increasing power in the legislature.

The line garnered titles more prestigious than a mere barony; and by dint of increasing wealth and influence, the "De Gabastons" finally secured an earldom (of "Thool") in their lineage and became "Degabastons" (this event under the reign of Hanoverians—those usurpers who were summoned by a pack of parliamentarian traitors into England from the blackest pit of the European continent specifically in order to subjugate all our island opposition to plutocracy, atheism, and devil-worship). Each one of the male line were damnably long-lived, with none perishing before achieving at least their eightieth year and successfully fathering children only in obscene old age; all other offspring from their loins had a mysterious habit of dying either in the womb or in early infancy.

And I say to you that the very nexus of the cult in England was consolidated in this place: in Thool Abbey, under the fiendish direction of Francis Degabaston, First Earl of Thool, born in late 1670. It was said his grandfather, Charles, Sixth Baron De Gabaston, died before the birth of Lord Francis's father, who is the missing link—this mysterious Seventh Baron, of whom almost all records have been subsequently obliterated or falsified. Such was the iniquity attached to his reputation that even his name itself is a matter of conjecture, but it is widely accepted the Seventh Baron was born sometime in 1597. My own researches uncovered obliquely fiendish indications of a most bewildering nature that reveal good reasons for his identity to have been obfuscated. There are hints not only that he had been deliberately buried alive, but also that his body had been, very shortly afterwards, exhumed by witch-finders; that he was found to be still alive in the grave; and that he had subsequently been burned at the stake (in 1648) as a wizard. Yet the sensational reports did not cease at that juncture. For it was rumoured he survived this ordeal, routed all his enemies, and lived on thereafter as a maimed, bitter hermit for a further twenty-two years, still practising his sorcery until his final death in the year 1670. It seems incredible that during this, the most iniquitous of periods in their history, to the ancient barony of De Gabaston was then added an earldom of Thool; but such are surely the vicissitudes of a nation governed by a godless Whiggism which now had the Crown wholly beneath its heel.

The nameless Seventh Baron's son, Lord Francis, then began his own abominations in the 1690s, and they reached their supreme height in the 1750s: the culmination of a blighted lineage by then riddled with venereal disease, habitual incest, and the tradition of the secret practice of sorcery. He died, mark you, in 1755, at the relatively modest age of eighty-five, but not before the heritage of festering degeneracy was passed on to his ghoulish, twisted-limbed heir, Gerald, the second Earl, he of an extraordinarily long life, who fathered a child with an idiot bride whilst in his eighty-sixth year; a scion who proved to be his only offspring—a female, born in 1840—one whose youthful mother was the same idiot bride who became Countess of Thool, and who was then returned, after the birth, to the private asylum whence she had originally come (and who also died there within three days from a ruptured blood vessel caused by her constant screaming). And the result of this freakish union of an octogenarian and an idiot bride?—why, she, that devil: Lady Caroline Degabaston.

All this I uncovered in my initial researches (and surely more horrible discoveries than those are to be made whilst rifling in graves), but even worse was to follow. For it became clear, as I continued to delve deeper, that her degenerate ancient father, Gerald, the second Earl (who did not die, so the records state, until 1860), had ample time before his death to instruct his daughter in the lore of the diabolic, and this unholy maid must have learnt much of the theory from his wizened lips and more of the practice of the blasphemously evil rituals he still conducted.

And so the malignancy was passed on from father to daughter, and although Lady Degabaston did not, of course, inherit the earldom (in fact, the title was extinct after the death of Gerald, the second Earl, there being no traceable male heirs in either direct or even ancillary branches), the freehold of Thool Abbey nevertheless passed to her. It was not contested even though no last will and testament by her father was known to be extant. After all, it was common knowledge that anyone who had previously dared cross the Degabastons, even in matters of negligible import, were quickly met by the most terrible of misfortunes.

There followed fourteen years of seclusion after the death of the second—and the last—of the Earls of Thool, fourteen years wherein Lady Degabaston shut herself away in the confines of the abbey, spurning all invitations and refusing all visitors; a secretive, long-serving family retinue of household servants possessed of singular unpleasantness and shrouded by ill-rumour formed her only contact with humanity.

There can be no doubt that the withdrawal of Lady Caroline Degabaston from society in the middle of the nineteenth century was for the purposes of perfecting some hideous occult rite her evil ancestors had themselves attempted with only partial success over the course of centuries. That the laws against witchcraft had been rendered impotent by a complacent and self-regarding philosophical cult of the "Enlightenment" in the eighteenth century (for atheism is the handmaiden, even if only unwittingly, of devilry, as I have already pointed out) proved very much to the advantage of the hellish Degabaston line.

What scant intelligence leaked out from locals living in the surrounding area during those damnable fourteen years was fantastical enough; accounts of strange multicoloured lights seen in the night-sky directly above the abbey, stories of tortured cries issuing from certain curiously deformed vegetation in isolated woodlands, discoveries of the graves of recent burials in churchyards having been sacrilegiously disturbed—*and seemingly from deep within the clay itself*—and yet all these suggestive factors were idly dismissed as the grossest of superstitious nonsense or as the recrudescence of some naggingly persistent "folklore." They were ruled "out of court" by a blinkered society utterly in thrall to the puerile dictates of Victorian "scientific" materialism. Once, in saner times—before our sense of the reality of the unseen world had dimmed—such a coordinated outbreak of witchcraft in England would have been swiftly checked by the gallows before it could gather its full momentum. Now, however, there was unleashed, unchecked, a pustulating blight of terrifying proportions—one of the most ferociously cancerous manifestations of spiritual hellishness on record: and one orchestrated to the full by the vile witch-cult of Thool Abbey.

And on Walpurgis Night 1874, Lady Caroline Degabaston was conceived of a child, one eight months later prematurely induced alive from the womb by abortionists on Christmas Day (so as to make the unnatural birth a vile mockery of the nativity of Our Lord and Savour).

The child was named Lilith, after that Babylonian night-demon Lilitu, who is, as you know, also the cursed Lilith of Talmudic lore—the spurned first wife of Adam, neither formed from out the clay nor formed like his second wife Eve from one of Adam's ribs. That the Lilith-demon was a fallen angel, or succubus, mother only to devils, and took the shape of a serpent in order to provoke the Fall of Man was, in any case, much in her favour (at least according to the principles of the wicked Gnostic sect of the Cathari, the so-called "pure ones," whose "purity" was fealty to the Principle of Subversion).

And, likewise, the child-Lilith's father was, without question, no mortal man, but some primal force summoned into this world by the infernal machinations of Lady Degabaston herself.

I searched tirelessly in multitudes of the incunabula housed in the closely guarded secret archives of the Vatican Library, but I could not uncover its name. For even amongst the half-obliterated papyri of the Monarchs of Hekau—that ancient cult that worshipped the principle of the Unspeakable and made child sacrifices to it—there is a shuddering reticence. But the principal, defining characteristic by which its mortal manifestations might be recognised is that of the attenuated white hands of deathly paleness with clutching fingers that, leech-like, feast upon the victim's blood.

Now, to return to the child-Lilith: it is clear to me the abominable hybrid was swiftly despatched to the outskirts of London, to Highgate Village, and (as was prearranged) there adopted by the Blake family of the parish. That the Blakes were themselves confederates of the Degabaston line you must not doubt, and they brought her up as if she were a foundling orphan. At least, that was the lie they told to the London society in which they moved.

It was only as a vessel for dark forces that the child was brought into existence: Lady Degabaston herself had no maternal feelings. Indeed, being of that nefarious witch-breed who favour abortion over motherhood, she would have been devoid of maternal compassion even had her child been fathered by a mortal husband or lover, rather than its being fathered by something Unspeakable.

Though utterly contemptuous of local gossip, Lady Degabaston had no wish to acknowledge Lilith publicly as her daughter; for then the question as to the child's parentage would have been raised. It was the purpose of the witch-cult to contaminate London itself using Lilith Blake as their catalyst. She communicated frequently with her mother, though not via commonplace channels; those who mastered the black art of telepathy have no need of recourse to pen and paper, or to telegrams and the like. At night, when their power is strongest, witches ride chariots of darkness into any sin-steeped dream.

And it was by this telepathic method Lady Degabaston schooled her daughter in the forbidden occult processes, guiding her in the actions that gained for Lilith Blake such a terrible notoriety in the literary *fin de siècle,* and her activities were more dangerous than the worst excesses of an Oscar Wilde, or even a Count Stenbock; for the influence of

those two personages was purely a consequence of trans-
gressing proprieties. Such dandies and decadents merely
shocked polite society when they played at wilful sinful-
ness, but as for Lilith Blake; *she was herself sin incarnate.*
She was at once irresistible and repulsive. To drive her ad-
mirers to self-destruction was the consummation she
sought; the merely carnal motive formed no part of her
purpose. Already, in life, there lingered about her some
sickening prefigurement of destiny; an unhallowed perfume
of charnel decay. Her debased conversation centred almost
exclusively around morbid topics no decent young woman
would essay; of lingering consciousness in the brains of
corpses, of unmentionable books which apparently wrote
themselves, and of the suicidal instructions secretly transmitted therein by revenants into the minds of unsuspecting
dreamers and passed off by them as mere fictions, until it
was far too late.

Naturally, the appearance in late 1895 of her slim collection of tales, *The Reunion and Others,* despite its limited
print-run, caused a minor sensation. You will recall its title
story, the ghastly account of the spectre of a long-fingered
murderess, a strangler of children in life, who haunts the
streets of London and whose appearances (invariably during rainstorms) cause all colour to drain out of the waking
world and render it a nightmare.

It was whispered, or so it was said, by a perspicacious
theologian with whom she came into contact that such a
hybrid abomination could not live for long; that her continued existence would be a defiance of Providence itself.
This same theologian must have breathed a sigh of relief
when, before she reached her twenty-second birthday, Lilith Blake was entombed within the sepulchre that had al-

ready been reared for her in the western grounds of Highgate Cemetery. Her ornate sepulchre had been paid for more than a year previously (in secret) by Lady Degabaston, upon the appearance of Lilith's collection of weird tales. The structure had been erected with unseemly haste, and had only served to increase local gossip at the time. A virulent stomach cancer was blamed by the Blake family as the cause of Lilith's death in 1896; but they themselves dispersed as soon as the funeral service was over and were subsequently heard of no more—their house in the village vacated, then shut and boarded up permanently, their part in the saga abruptly terminated.

The further scandal attached to that nocturnal funeral service only added to the ghastliness of the legend. My eyewitness, the same theologian, said it was a ceremony presided over by a "priest" of indeterminate denomination, one cowled and unbelievably ancient; whose features were curiously lopsided and whose bloodshot left eye glistened crimson by lamplight while a band of driving rain lashed down over the macabre tableau. He intoned a strange rite in a language unknown to the one curious onlooker, and as for the handful of actual mourners in attendance, well, such was their outré, outdated apparel and ghastly appearance they might have crawled out from coffins across the subterranean locality specifically in order to pay their final respects.

Now I must hasten to my conclusion.

It is my belief this "funeral" ceremony was an elaborate ruse concealing another ceremony; one of hideous import. Lilith Blake had not suddenly died of cancer as was claimed by her guardians; rather, she deliberately extinguished her own life. I suspect she did so through an overdose of laudanum or some other drug but, in any case, *it was in order to further her own and the Degabastons' scheme that she embraced death; for suicide has certain infernal advantages.*

You will recall my experiences in 1913, those experiences that postdate her entombment by seventeen years. You will also recall my allusion to the hidden arcana and practice of auto-necromancy, passed down through generations of the Degabaston line. The so-called funeral ceremony was nothing of the sort; it was some primal precursor of the Black Mass, a rite carried out in intercession for the sorcery upon which the dead Lilith Blake was now already wholly engaged.

It is my contention Lilith Blake has continued to be in telepathic contact with her mother Lady Caroline Degabaston since the former's "death" in 1896. She has been pouring out the secrets of hell from her grave by this means ever since.

I believe the entire disgusting state of affairs was planned from the very beginning; that it dates back centuries and only now has achieved the perfection of the hideously grotesque. I also believe that the story of a so-called cancerous affliction in her stomach hints at a further reproductive experiment which is very much in accordance with the warped traditions of the Degabastons.

And it was during later research, undertaken for a sequel to my book *The Damnable Cult of Witchcraft,* that the particulars of a signed and inscribed copy of *The Reunion and Others* were brought to my attention; a copy whose inscription, not meant to be seen by anyone outside the clan, validated all my worst suspicions. It was to confirm the details that I sought admission to Thool Abbey and, in so doing, to expunge the forces of darkness through exorcism.

With regard to the inscription in the book *The Reunion and Others,* my informant who saw it in Thool Abbey advised me that it ran as follows, though, of course, I have not yet seen it with my own eyes:

To LADY CAROLINE DEGABASTON, Mother OF HARLOTS AND ABOMINATIONS OF THE EARTH, MYSTERY, BABYLON THE GREAT—from HER daughter LILITH whose own womb now engenders the Word of darkness.

# Chapter Seven

Proprieties of place, and especially of time, are the bugbears that terrify mankind from the contemplation of the magnificent.
—EDGAR A. POE, "The Assignation" (1844)

He has cast you forth into the outer darkness, where everlasting ruin awaits you and your abettors. —From the *Rituale Romanum* of the Catholic Church

During the course of listening to the Revd. Winters's long verbal narrative I had expected that some attempt might be made upon the barricaded door by the denizens of the abbey in order to gain admittance and seize the two of us. But no such attempt was made. I supposed therefore that, while darkness reigned, they were the masters of the situation. Both of us were now their prisoners, and their previous mode of action seemed to indicate they favoured a long, drawn-out campaign of attrition—and of stealthy caution—rather than any swift dénouement.

I felt a sense of genuine repentance at my initial, hasty misjudging of the Revd. Winters. It was now evident to me that he too had suffered, body and soul, just as greatly as I had myself. His knowledge had not been won simply through theory and book-learning; the gates of hell had opened up in his own life and he had experienced the depths of damnation which lay beyond them.

"You mentioned a particular informant who was also an eyewitness," I said. "What was his name?"

"The theologian George L. Burgess; he it was who was present at the entombment of Lilith Blake in 1896 and he it was

who, in addition, travelled in 1903 to the icy northern waste-
lands of the European continent searching for Thomas Ariel,
author of the fabled *Kruptos*. Managing to obtain, through deception, some thirty-eight volumes of that *magnum opus* while
acting as an agent for Lady Degabaston, he brought them back
here to Thool Abbey. I met him on several occasions in 1929, by
which time he had fully renounced the devil and all his works.
Up until then, he had been playing a dangerous game; for the
sake of advancing his understanding of the esoteric, he had
been an agent both for darkness and light. There are great perils in such intellectual vanity. A grey twilight of neutrality cannot long persist: one or other force must ultimately triumph."

"You have heard nothing from him since 1929?" I said.

"Nothing. He has apparently vanished off the face of the
earth," he said. "It is, of course, possible that the fiends here
now have him back in their clutches."

A look of pained remorse crossed his features as he uttered
the words, and I realised he harboured a sense of responsibility
for what might have been the sorry fate of George Burgess. Had
the man escaped the influence of Lady Degabaston in later life
and found a measure of liberty as a fugitive, only for his association with Winters to result in his being drawn once more into
the infernal spider-web of Thool Abbey?

"Do you know how long you yourself have been kept prisoner here? When did you first arrive at Thool Abbey?" Winters
said, framing a question which I had sought to push to the
back of my mind.

He was eyeing me with a searching gaze, and I felt self-
conscious about my appearance. His quizzical stare suggested
he believed me to be much older than I was. I had already noticed the proliferation of new lines and deep furrows upon my
face, the tiredness that crept up upon me during sustained

bodily exertion, and the falling out of a number of my teeth. The abbey itself sucked the life out of its inhabitants, preternaturally ageing them beyond their actual years, and my own sense of time was so distorted I could not hope to chart its actual passage with any degree of accuracy. I knew when first I arrived at the abbey I was forty-three years of age.

"I arrived in October 1940," I replied, finally, the exact date beyond my powers of recall.

"The date is now the tenth of August 1948," Revd. Winters said.

Almost eight years as a prisoner! I might as well have been comatose all that time, since I knew nothing of what had transpired in the outside world.

"How goes the war?" I said. The question sounded strange upon my lips; I had given little thought to the momentous events that must have played out across Europe during the period of my incarceration.

"The war has been over for three years. Europe is lost."

"To the National Socialists?"

"No, not to them, to those other heathens; to the International Socialists."

"What of Britain?"

"Britain is in their hands too; bankrupted, under severe rationing, with her Empire shrinking back to its centre."

I tried to question him further, but he raised one of his kid-gloved hands in protest and immediately returned to the peril in our present situation.

"No attempt has been made by the devils in this place to storm our barricade and gain admittance to this chamber. I must undertake countermeasures against the evil in Thool Abbey. If they are marshalling their forces then we must strike before they can do so," he said.

"What do you propose?" I replied. "You still insist upon attempting an exorcism?"

"Firstly I desire sight of that copy of *The Reunion and Others* in the abbey library and, once my suspicions are confirmed, then yes, it will be exorcism. You will assist in the ceremony by reading the responses," he said. "Follow my lead and do not listen to anything else. The devil is the father of lies."

"An exorcism will be futile. I tell you, the only thing to do is to burn down the whole abbey, starting with the library."

He stiffened again, snorted dismissively through his nose, and glanced around the room in confusion, evidently seeking for some important item he had misplaced.

"I cannot locate my small valise. It contains the necessary accoutrements. The *Rituale Romanum,* holy water, and the purple stole. I must have put it down outside the door when I passed you the key to this room."

We removed the improvised barricade as swiftly and quietly as we were able and, sure enough, outside in the passageway there was a black-leather valise. The Revd. Winters picked it up and made his way cautiously along the corridor, holding a candle in his other fist, wax dribbling onto the glove. He looked back over his shoulder, inclining his head for me to follow. I trailed after him, loping crab-like with my walking cane, certain that all we were about to do was to attempt to extinguish a furnace with drops of water.

We were unmolested during our passage through the winding corridors and stairwells of the interior, though on several occasions we took false turnings; and it seemed to me the architecture of the abbey had subtly reorganised itself in a manner calculated to baffle us. Nevertheless, we found our way through leagues of darkness to the great hall and from there passed through the low arched door into the abbey library.

The Revd. Winters gave utterance to a startled cry, for he had advanced ahead of me into the chamber and saw inside before me.

The hunched figure of Lady Degabaston awaited us there, seated at the central table next to a lit candelabrum, attired in her customary voluminous black dress of antique design, with dotted veil and black-lace mantilla. One of her pale, claw-like hands, with gnarled bony fingers, its back speckled with liver-spots, rested on an open volume. She slowly raised her head as we entered fully into the library and then she croaked out the following words:

"Welcome, at long last, to Thool Abbey, Reverend," she said.

"Your Ladyship," he replied, formally inclining his head, his voice somewhat strangled. "You are doubtless fully cognisant of the real reason for my presence."

He set the valise down on a corner of the table, within easy reach. Sweat oozed from his forehead, displacing white powder, revealing pinkish skin beneath.

She chuckled, mirthlessly and iniquitously, and, with a sudden convulsive movement, the book slid towards us, of its own accord, across the width of the table.

It was that personalised copy of *The Reunion and Others,* open at the title page, and sure enough, it bore the inscription the Revd. Winters had already described to me:

To LADY CAROLINE DEGABASTON, Mother OF HARLOTS AND ABOMINATIONS OF THE EARTH, MYSTERY, BABYLON THE GREAT—from HER daughter LILITH whose own womb now engenders the Word of darkness.

"I must put you to the question," the Revd. Winters said.

A wheezing issued from beneath her veil as her dried-up lungs sucked in air.

"When was the word of darkness torn by you from its grave-womb?"

An exhalation of breath, bearing a fetid stench, polluted the space between accused and accuser.

"1897."

"And she calls to you even now, down there in the depths, gestating further offspring, but this time outside the womb?"

A monstrous snarl, like the howl of those beasts in the woodlands. Then this declamation, the last word uttered in a roar:

"My own hands are not sufficient to the task, but you know THIS."

They were exchanging allusions I was unable to follow with complete clarity, though I realised that their subject was undoubtedly Lilith Blake and her *post mortem* influence upon worldly events.

"And so you have aided that foul daughter of yours in recent attempts to put me to use as an intermediary—as her *scribe*," he said.

Her voice replied in a deep bass tone, one generated from far down in her throat, and her former croaking and wheezing were banished; it was as if she were gaining infernal strength from the confrontation.

"You were contaminated once before, foolish priest, and do not think such trespasses are so easily forgiven and washed away," she said. "You were baptised in *our* blood."

"I was sincere in my repentance—nothing can keep out the forgiveness of Our Lord and Saviour from those who are truly contrite," the Revd. Winters responded.

"Have you permission from your bishop to attempt an exorcism?"

He was now faltering. His lips were deathly white. The colour had drained from his face. He no longer had need of white powder to mask his unusually florid complexion.

"Don't listen to her!" I shouted. "You are falling under her spell!"

He turned to me, gave another of those curious smiles, and nodded. Then he reached for the valise and unclasped it, preparing to undertake the rite of exorcism. As he did so, Lady Degabaston rose from her seat, drawing herself up to a fully standing position.

From the shadows at the back of the library, there emerged a hideous, twisted thing dressed in the eighteenth-century garb of periwig, frock coat, and breeches. It was ancient beyond belief, with yellow, parchment-like skin stretched over a grinning death's-head. Deeply sunken, cobalt-coloured eyes peered out from the depths of the skull sockets.

"I have the honour to present to you both, gentlemen, my father, Gerald, Second Earl of Thool," Lady Degabaston said as her voice abruptly resumed its croaky, wheezing timbre.

The nobleman-lich beside her essayed a mocking bow with a courtly flourish. Aristocratic scorn lay behind the gesture.

I had no real confidence in the efficacy of an exorcism, but nevertheless I was prepared to try anything in order to dispel the fresh nightmare that was engulfing both myself and the Revd. Winters. I turned away from the filthy apparition of the Earl and back to my ally the priest, and wondered why he hesitated to begin the ceremony. Had his reason finally tottered under the strain? Or had the Degabaston spell of evil mastered him? He stood there immobile, rigid as a mediaeval statue.

And then I saw that the open valise was empty. They had removed its contents in advance of our confronting them down here, and had doubtless done so shortly after we had barricaded ourselves in my attic chamber.

Another member of the retinue now stepped forward from the shadows, and the Revd. Winters staggered and then clutched at the edge of the table for support as he beheld its withered and sunken—yet still recognisable—features. I did not need to be told the identity of this person; for I had guessed the moment the priest had laid eyes on him, though my supposition was immediately confirmed.

"Burgess," Winters then whispered, "is it really you?"

The witch-cult had long been at work upon the theologian's emaciated carcass, and it was apparent not only that he had indeed been recaptured in 1929 but also that he had been kept alive after death in order for them to perfect a hellish level of suffering upon him. His eyes had been removed and their lids sewn open so that empty sockets stared sightlessly, without cessation, at nothingness. Burgess—or what was left of him—did not speak, did not reply, to Winters's query.

And in his grasp he held all the accoutrements Winters had required for the exorcism: the Roman Ritual, the purple stole, and the phial of holy water. But the book was burnt, its pages blackened, the stole was torn and shredded, and the phial had been poured out and emptied.

"Speak up," Lady Degabaston said, as Burgess shuffled forward, his insect-thin legs threatening to buckle even under the negligible weight of his skeletal frame.

She reached over, cupped his mouth with her bony, claw-like hand, and forced open his jaws, holding up the candelabrum above the orifice so we could see clearly there was only a void within it, all the teeth gone, but, more pertinently, also that the tongue was torn out at its very root.

"A chastisement worthy of your own religion's Torquemada, don't you think?" Lady Degabaston wheezed. "Mayhap he wished to advise you that Thomas Ariel and the six million volumes of his *Kruptos* have been subjected to our version of the *auto-da-fé*."

From out the depths of the shadows in the library, the other dozen or so members of her retinue suddenly appeared, amongst them the bony myrmidon and Dr Cressop, who then held both myself and the still-struggling Revd. Winters firm in their clutches.

"You have yet more work to do for us," she said, addressing me, "but I have had quite enough of this mewling Catholic oaf who refuses to obey the instructions of my daughter. Remove his gloves."

With the utterance of those last words the Revd. Winters, now in a veritable frenzy, redoubled his efforts to break free from the denizens; but it was all in vain, for they pawed and tore anew at him, raising his arms to the level of his chest and then pulling off the kid-gloves that he had worn the entire time he had been at the abbey, revealing his bare hands.

I was baffled and amazed; for, even by flickering candle-light, I could not account for the sight: surely those hands could not be a part of any man's physical form? They were wholly feminine; the most delicate and lovely hands I had ever seen, the attenuated fingers of extraordinary grace and length. And they were absolutely white—whiter than the purest snow.

This wonderment yielded to horror in the space of a heart-beat, for, in the next instant, those beautiful yet alien hands—so incongruously attached to the Revd. Winters's wrists!—took on a life of their own; and the long, leech-like fingers suddenly writhed with inconceivable agitation. The abbey retinue responded as one to this development by standing back from the priest as if this vivification were a prearranged signal.

Then the white hands wrapped themselves around the throat of the Revd. Winters—acting wholly independently of his will. The sight was grotesque; it was both ridiculous and appalling; and yet, before my very eyes the priest began strangling himself to death.

Lady Degabaston celebrated this hideous development by clapping together her own useless, arthritic claws, providing applause for the spectacle.

"Such wonderful twins!" she wheezed.

It was Dr Cressop who carried me away from the abbey library. I was dazed and incoherent, for the strain had been too keen on my already shattered nerves. He guided me up along the flights of stairs and through the cobwebby maze of corridors until I found myself lowered onto my bunk in the attic room high up in the Jacobean annexe of the abbey.

"I should like to impress upon you the fact Lady Degabaston is pleased with your progress," he said. "In particular, she remarked upon the fascination that your bibliography holds for her."

"It is no bibliography. It contains meaningless gibberish," I said.

"Only on the surface, I assure you. A close, attentive reader is always prepared to distinguish between a facile exoteric appearance and a more profound esoteric reality."

"Why don't you write such books yourselves?"

He held up both of his pitiful, claw-like hands in response.

"Would that we were capable of doing so!" Dr Cressop complained. "But we all labour under the same physical disadvantages, and are thus obliged to rely upon amanuenses like you for assistance. Nevertheless, we dictate what is to be written down."

"I reserve the right to censor, or even to obliterate, the results."

"I fear that your former associate, the Revd. Winters, reasoned likewise. Perhaps he will come around to our way of
thinking—as did Mr Burgess in the end—but then again perhaps not . . . Still, if not, he may find residence in the woodlands a refreshing change."

I was in total despair.

"Let me out of here."

"No, no, no," he replied, a frown crossing his scar-riven and
wrinkled features. "That wouldn't do at all. You don't seem to
understand yet just how much we value you and how delighted
we are to number you amongst our neophytes. Now you must
get some sleep, young man, for you have had quite an exciting
day. Doctor's orders, you know."

# Chapter Eight

People think that the totality of their knowledge depends on the nature and capacity to be known of the objects of knowledge. But this is all wrong. Everything that is known is comprehended not according to its own nature, but according to the ability to know of those who do the knowing . . . So it is that this divine fore-knowledge does not change the nature and property of things; it simply sees things that are its present exactly as they will happen at some time as future events.—ANICIUS MANLIUS SEVERINUS BOE-THIUS, *De Consolatione Philosophiae*, Book V

Shortly after the imposed "self-destruction" of the Revd. Winters, as I lay prostrate upon the dank sheets of my bunk, alone in the attic room and recovering my strength subsequent to my recent ordeal, a thunderstorm arose in the night. I first detected the distant rumble approaching from a great distance—the advent of a mighty tumult which ultimately silenced even the continual baying of the teratological monsters of the woodlands. Then there came wave after wave of rain mingled with hailstones. As the storm reached its peak, the wind picked up in force, becoming a howling gale, while the cataclysmic downpour buffeted the panes of my oriel window. I felt as if I were a passenger aboard some ancient timber ship that was caught in the ferocity of a tremendous storm at sea, the vessel lost in the endless, churning expanse of a blackly Stygian ocean. And I, who had longed for illumination, was now nearly blinded by the frequency and intensity of burst after burst of lightning flashes.

The rumbling detonations reminded me of the air-raid bombings over London that—or so the Revd. Winters had claimed—lay several years ago in the past, and I could not help also associating the sound with thoughts of warfare of another kind: warfare not temporal but spiritual; of Lucifer cast out of heaven with thunderbolts, of the fall of the rebel angels and of their subsequent transformation into demons. And then my mind further strayed back to that thing I must have read by the Revd. Winters: his encyclopedia of hell on earth, *The Damnable Cult of Witchcraft*. For I recalled the old tales of witches raising tempests whilst working at their ceremonies—a vile demonstration of their current power over a fallen universe, that power which the descendants of Adam and Eve had lost through original sin, but which the descendants of Cain and Lilitu the demon-Queen had illicitly regained through the worship of evil.

I wished (God forgive me!) for a dose of the soothing amber-coloured potion to quell my intolerable sense of foreboding and would even have welcomed the sight of the grisly Dr Cressop's arrival (had he borne with him the provider of dreamless sleep), but my agonies were not thus relieved. Instead, the thunderstorm went on and on for hours, until I was forced to muffle the din and blot out the flashes of light by burying my head in the musty confines of the pillows on my bunk.

I should have imagined it impossible to fall asleep unawares under such extreme circumstances, but the concatenation of my own tortured, circular thoughts, of my brain desiring relief from them, and, finally, of the sheer exhaustion wrought upon me by lack of proper rest, combined to cause me to slip gradually into deep slumber.

And in that episode of sleep, which could not be a dreamless one (for I had not imbibed the potion of Dr Cressop beforehand), there then arose a phantasmagoria of nightmarish proportions that threatened to engulf my reason forever.

I was surely in the same dream endured by the Revd. Winters—the dream which had been transmitted telepathically into his brain when he had first come under the evil influence of
the Thool Witch-Cult. The landscape of this dream was as described by him when he had recounted it to me during our
long, last discussion. And my sensations were as one who is not
moving through the past, the present, or the future but rather
as seen through that underlying aspect of eternity by which
time itself is sustained.

In this dream I was stumbling with my cane through a
maze of sunken pathways in a hillside cemetery at twilight with
a yellow miasma of ground-mist drifting around at knee-
height. I knew I was lost and terrified; terrified not because I
was in flight from some horror, but rather because that same
horror was insidiously drawing me closer despite my efforts to
evade it. The multitude of decrepit open-doored tombs and rifled, upturned graves told me that the occupants had burst
forth from centuries of charnel captivity. They now stalked
abroad on the malefic errands ordered by a nexus of evil which
had projected its telepathic tendrils into those rotted carcasses.

Eventually, after hacking my way through the undergrowth
and a barrier of immense bramble bushes, I found myself in a
veritable amphitheatre of sycamore trees and, at its core, there
stood the huge, gaunt tomb of Lilith Blake. It seemed to stand
out from its surroundings with a phosphorescent intensity in the
twilight, as if the very decay of its masonry had infused the
structure with life—the type of abnormally virulent bacterial life
which only flourishes once decomposition sets into a dead body.

I observed the green marble tablet bearing the epitaph of
its occupant but found simply the words "Lilith Blake. Born 25
December 1874 . . ." The other date, that of her death, had been
utterly obscured by a motley streak of red lichen that had

snaked up from beyond the stairs of the underground vault to the marble tablet on the side. I scraped off the lichen using the tip of my cane only to discover the remainder of the tablet beneath had been effaced. The once-elaborate finials were now little more than corroded stumps; as incongruous as bejewelled fingers on a leper. And at the front of the tomb, where I had expected to find the peaked trellis gateway hanging ajar (as was the case with all the entrances to other tombs I had seen within the necropolis), this one, to the contrary, was closed.

The urge to descend and attempt to somehow wrench open that gate grew upon me the longer I stood there gazing downwards at the aperture. I recalled how the Revd. Winters had told me of his own wicked desire to enter into the inner crypt wherein the undying corpse of Lilith Blake lay and to join with her in a monstrous subterranean eternity of hell. Finally, the tomb proffered an invitation to me, for, with an eerie screech of rusted hinges, the trellised gateway swung open of its own accord. Still I fought to gain mastery over my urge to descend, and I planted my cane on the ground in front of me, sinking its tip into the mist-covered soil at my feet, shutting my eyes and willing myself desperately to wake up from the all-encompassing nightmare.

I thought I heard once more the booming detonations of that thunderstorm in the outside world, the world beyond this dream, and, even with my eyes closed, seemed again to detect the far-off flashes of lightning still striking across the vast estate of Thool Abbey. Yet before I could will myself back to full, waking consciousness, I heard a voice calling to me from the inner depths, a musical voice that uttered meaningless words of intolerable ecstasy; words that were the very soul of poetry itself, but a fiendish poetry which turned to infinite evil as its beauty, words which hinted at the incomparable bliss of the suspended putrescence to be found in conscious death. The now-distant detonations and the dim flashes of the thunderstorm in the waking world gradually died away as I listened to those words, and I opened my eyes to gaze once more at the open trellis gateway, at its red-lichen covered flight of steps, and at the entranceway into the underground vault, whence the source of the melodiously damnable siren-call emanated.

The Revd. Winters had turned away when upon the threshold that led down to stupendous revelations and then returned to the bosom of the church. But he had been born a Catholic, and I had not; and, after all, what good had his shrinking from the brink and reconciling with his church done him? Had he not been drawn back into the same web years later and met with destruction in Thool Abbey just the same?

I could not be sure these thoughts were entirely my own. Even deep within the dream I was aware that my free-will was in peril of corruption from outside interference. My thoughts—I insist—were entirely clear, yet in that clarity there was no guarantee they were of my volition. I had now passed the stage of feeling any urge or compulsion to act other than in a manner that I myself believed I wished to act. I had asked for no sign that I had not gone mad in this dream, but surely I had been vouchsafed one in the form of the crystalline nature of my deliberations.

And so I began my descent, crab-like, with my cane, taking care upon the lichen-mottled flight of steps, passing through the trellis gateway, over the threshold of the tomb, and down the increasingly nitre-choked, cramped, interior corkscrew stairway that led into the bowels of the earth and terminated only at the crypt of Lilith Blake. And as I descended I saw with even more clarity despite the omnipresent gloom, for the spectral range of my vision increased until, finally, darkness itself seemed to possess an iridescent quality.

The subterranean journey down the winding staircase to the abominable chamber at its base was one of stifling discomfort; of feverish claustrophobia, with the all-encompassing walls of the vertical passageway always within reach, the air foetid with the aroma of decay and mould, its tangy stench thick in my nostrils. Around my feet and cane wriggled vilely bloated grave-worms, bleached utterly white by their underground existence, rendered blind, ravening for the rotting dead—which ghoulish sustenance the Lilithean arcana of suspended decomposition had provided for them.

All the while, as I descended, there was that musical voice calling to me from the inner depths of darkness, welling up from below, urging me with insistent clamour, still uttering words of intolerable ecstasy; words that had ceased to be meaningless, words which explicitly promised to me alone the incomparable, hellish bliss that was to be found in the endless aeons of consciousness-in-death that only she, Lilith Blake, could provide. And so, finally, I reached the foot of the dizzying shaft that had been sunk far below the tomb of that vast hillside necropolis and I entered into her low, vaulted burial chamber, my mind in a pacified state of total obeisance; and then the musical voice with its words of irresistible lyricism and hideous ecstasy abruptly ceased, leaving a gaunt silence in its wake.

As I stared about me, I could not help but marvel at this burial chamber, and at the macabre feat of Victorian engineering that had brought it into subterranean existence. I experienced a jolt of amazement of no less an order than the fabulous jolt of amazement reported by Howard Carter in the celebrated excavation in The Valley of the Kings when first he gained entrance to the lost tomb of the Pharaoh Tutankhamen. Truly, there were certain ironic parallels to be made between that boy-king and Lilith Blake. Had not both rulers surrounded themselves with a series of personal objects and effects, precious to them in life, and which were, after death, buried along with them? Although the crypt of Lilith Blake could not boast of a multitude of treasures consisting of merely venal gold or silver, nevertheless the charnel items she valued were doubtless equally as important in her own realm of morbid telepathic dreams, and were, as I soon discovered, monstrously suggestive of her evil design to pass all eternity in an undead state. So, too, did not the Pharaoh arrange to have his own corpse prepared—made incorruptible to decay—in order that his soul might safely return to it after voyaging through the afterlife as envisaged in the Egyptian Book of the Dead?

You will have already realised in advance of my stating it expressly what items actually constituted the "treasures" in the crypt of Lilith Blake: they were, of course, comprised chiefly of hundreds of books, of all shapes and sizes, of all bindings and ages, stacked into tottering piles reaching upwards to the vaulted ceiling. One had to pick one's path carefully through the narrow aisles that were formed solely by their absence, and my gaze fell upon the spines of some three or four dozen of the volumes as I sought out the centre of the musty bibliophilic labyrinth.

Of the titles which I saw on the spines of those books many were utterly unfamiliar to me (though all were worded with evil nomenclature), yet there were many others which were appallingly familiar—the latter both from recent time spent in the diabolic library of Thool Abbey and also by recollection of the most ill-regarded of the items which had passed through my hands whilst I had been employed cataloguing in the dank,

gaslit basement of the antiquarian bookshop situated in an al-
ley in Hampstead Village.

Lilith Blake had doubtless been entombed with her entire
library; and yet, with bewilderment, I could not help but also
note there were books present in that crypt which bespoke of
an anachronistic discrepancy. Did not some of them postdate
her death in 1896? Had they then been deposited down here
subsequently as tributes, or offerings, by a faithful servitor or
attendant, such as the priestly ancient with the crimson left eye
who had reputedly presided over her curious internment ceremony? Or was it the case that the suspension of bodily decay
interfered, in some localised manner, with the passage of time
in that portion of the outside world which was within range of
her telepathic powers? Had she formed, by the arcana of auto-
necromancy, a corresponding suspension of the laws of time
and space, an overflowing of her energies, a specific *genius loci*?
What, too, of the red lichen that had eaten away the date of her
death on that memorial plaque? More than ever, I was conscious of being subject to the dream of some irresistible outside
agency or force. And most maddeningly of all, I could not
shake off the impression that, though glimpsed only from the
corners of my eyes, there were two huge and thin white spiders
crawling stealthily over and between the stacks of books, each
of them moving upon five limbs.

Yet even as these speculations and distractions raged
through my senses in bewildering profusion, I did not lose
sight of my central objective; the spell of that bewitching
summons to gaze upon her—in the flesh—had already too
deeply embedded itself in my brain to be denied. And all hesi-
tation dissipated entirely when I found myself standing before
the coffin which contained the body of Lilith Blake and saw
that the lid had already been removed, perhaps waiting to be

replaced. It stood almost upright close by, having been leant against one of the many impromptu columns formed of the dusty volumes from her personal library. The open coffin rested upon a stone plinth of waist-height, one embellished with a certain armorial crest, containing esoteric symbols I could not identify.

It was scarcely a funeral casket worthy of housing her remains; and certainly no Egyptian sarcophagus wrought in elaborate splendour as the vessel to ferry a Pharaoh through the afterlife. The wooden boards of the sides of the oblong box were deep, obscuring its occupant from immediate view, and I was repulsed by the smell of the dank patches of mould that had spawned upon the surface. In order to see within I had to approach right up to the edge of the opening, and draw myself up to my full height upon my tiptoes. My cane assisted in my maintaining my balance, for I settled the grip-end of it upon the ledge of the plinth, using it as a lever.

That my vision was supernaturally altered to accommodate itself to darkness, I have already pointed out, and my sole mental refuge against the abomination I saw within the coffin is the possibility that this abnormal increase in my spectral range (resulting in increased distortion as a side-effect) might just account for what I saw—or what I thought I saw—or perhaps what I was deceived into seeing.

Resting in the casket was a female figure clothed in a soot-blackened muslin shroud. Her partially singed (yet still for the most part intact and raven-black) hair had grown down to her waist during the long period of entombment, and such was the arrangement of those long tresses that they entirely covered the hands (which I had been so curious to see) folded across her bosom, and thus hid them from my view. Would that those tresses had also covered her face! As it was, the hair was parted high upon her forehead, revealing the full, nightmarish vision of the countenance of Lilith Blake. My thoughts were of some act of recent desecration, of some infinitely decadent necro-phile who delighted in disfiguring the dead with fire, but then I recalled the age-old ultimate remedy against witches—that of their purging by flames.

Would that the macabre arsonist had completed his work—whether that work had been undertaken in the name of purity or perversity—and would that he had utterly destroyed the thing that now lay there in the coffin by reducing it to nothing but ashes! For what remained was too much of a grotesque parody of the formerly beauteous creature that she, Lilith Blake, was reputed to have been. The charred, disfigured face had been hideously burnt; its actual features were scarcely rec-ognisable. The entire lower half and most of the right side up to the temple, including the flesh of the nose, the lips, and the chin (yet it was not so with her closed eyes with their spidery lashes!), was seared away down to the skull—and her mouth bore the sardonic grin of the death's-head with teeth that were small, yellowed and sharp.

Yet there is one particular I have not yet touched upon when it comes to my delineating all the aspects of the ravaged form that rested in the coffin.

It is a particular aspect of supremely twisted irony; for there could be no doubt, given the distended curve of her navel, that Lilith Blake bore some progeny in her womb. Such was its pro-found distension that it might even have contained more than one festering offspring. Whether this progeny was conceived before or after her demise, I could not tell, but that something had grown close to its full term inside her whilst Blake had been entombed within this charnel-house seemed a supposition impossible to avoid. And it was only when her blank, loathsome eyes blinked open and stared straight into my own that I stupidly realised damage sufficient to put an end to a living person could not terminate the existence of a thing that had long since transcended the gulf between the realms of life and death, of space and time, and of existence and non-existence.

A coherent account of my further experiences is almost impossible from this juncture. I knew I was trapped in a dream or in someone else's dream (though surely not that of the Revd. Winters, for I had gone farther than he by descending into the very crypt of Lilith Blake); but it was after this point that my experiences took on the surrealistic, non-linear pattern of derangement, as if I had incontrovertibly gone mad inside that unearthly dream. Yet I must attempt to impart what information I can, even if it be inchoate, lest certain suggestive points within those further experiences be lost to futurity.

I felt I was being throttled and suffocated by the five spindly limbs of those two huge white spiders that had fastened themselves upon my face and throat respectively; and these things were glutting themselves upon my lifeblood. Yet at the same time, they were also flooding my mind with intimations of a yet greater nightmare-world. I can only partially—by suggestion and the weak associative power of metaphor—convey my absolute belief that these huge white spiders were also the hands of Lilith Blake, hands that had been used to write of inconceivable horrors *whilst she was entombed,* and the products of these labours were not merely accounts of supernatural phenomena, but were actually supernatural phenomena in themselves. And that Blake worked upon some collection of fictional episodes designed not to stimulate thought, not to liberate thought, but to enslave it, to merge the thoughts of the cursed dead-who-do-not-die with the thoughts of those still living, to conjure up absolute evil in the shape of an all-consuming privation that thwarted life, *even within the womb,* had been the scheme of the witch-cult all along.

The progeny that would be ultimately removed from Lilith Blake's uterus would not be a human child, nor some hybrid of demon and human, *as she herself was,* but rather the thing with which she was initially buried—the thing of crumpled black leather whose once-blank pages of vellum she filled in the darkness of that book-lined crypt, delineating the dreaming of her dreams while in suspended decay, the thing that she herself had penned in her own blood, and which one of her servitors had then stitched up inside her desiccated womb for a period of further internal gestation after the accursed thing was finally begotten; the book whose title was *The White Hands.* And this was not the end of the process, for after it was unnaturally birthed into the world it would continue to evolve further, into ever more hideous, unimaginable forms of privation.

The two huge, five-limbed white spiders squeezed more tightly around my throat and mouth, having brought me telepathically to this point of appalling realisation, and just before I inwardly shrieked my way out of the dream and back into the waking world in a veritable paroxysm of terror, I had a final impression that there was something even more nightmarish I had not quite grasped but which, had I done so, would have resulted in ultimate insanity.

I awoke, now unfettered, having shrieked myself up from those catacombs of dream, to gain full consciousness lying upon my bunk in the attic room of the Jacobean annexe of Thool Abbey, my body drenched in sweat and my heart pounding in my chest. Finally, after much effort, I managed to gain some measure of control over myself and staggered to the oriel window. The late tempest had subsided and the distant rumble of thunder, the heavy rain, and the flashing storm clouds rolled rapidly away into the shadows of the west. As it did so, the howling from the woodlands gradually recommenced. At first in only isolated instances, but, eventually, as a long, drawn-out, sustained chorus.

Upon the bureau there lay a pair of crumpled, familiar kid-gloves that had belonged to my friend. I feared for the first signs of any alteration in my own hands, the telltale bleaching of the skin, the steady lengthening of the fingers, the start of that process would surely mean I was nearing the end of sanity. And so, not without a sense of my own cowardice, I slipped the gloves over my hands, hiding them from sight.

I lit a candle and held it up, for one of the hump-backed teratological monsters had wandered from the woods, its deformed, red-lichen-mottled grey bulk snuffling about the sickly growth of the untended lawn, persistent in a search for something it had perhaps lost.

As if alerted by the feeble source of light from my window, it raised its head from the thick ground-mist and I saw what appeared to be the distorted, despairing face of the Revd. Winters looking up at me—a face that tapered to a monstrous snout; but the distance between us was great, darkness was again closing in, my thoughts were utterly disordered by the nightmare from which I had just awakened, and so I could not be certain.

# Chapter Nine

But the dream-horror which I speak of is far more frightful. The dreamer finds housed within himself—occupying, as it were, some separate chamber in his brain—holding, perhaps, from that station a secret and detestable commerce with his own heart—some horrid alien nature. What if it were his own nature repeated,—still, if the duality were distinctly perceptible, even *that*—even this mere numerical double of his own consciousness—might be a curse too mighty to be sustained.—THOMAS DE QUINCEY

No longer was I held prisoner in that attic room high up in the Jacobean annexe. With the disposal of the Revd. Alphonsus Winters, my liberty was restored—or rather partially so—for I was free to wander only within the abbey and around its immediate environs. In any case, thoughts of making another escape attempt did not work their way to the forefront of my mind, and I was overpowered by a sense of restless lethargy and defeatism. Darkness again reigned inviolate.

It seemed entirely possible that the teratological monsters which populated the woodlands had once been interlopers from the outside world and had intruded upon Thool Abbey and its environs, seeking to thwart the witch-cult's satanic designs, and had thus aroused its wrath. But some of the monsters may also have once been persons whom they had sought to marshal to their wickedness—perhaps to maintain the requisite number of thirteen—and yet the coven had failed in attempts to convert these individuals. They, then, like myself, had doubtless tried to effect an escape from the clutches of the witch-cult. If this were so, then the Degabastons and their evil associates had been lenient thus far with me; for I had made such escape attempts on two occasions already, and perhaps to do so for a third time would result in the same ultimate chastisement of a most stupefyingly horrible nature. But, of course, I had also been informed by Dr Cressop that I was still of particular use to them and expected (with a dread I can scarcely communicate) to be returned to my enforced labours in the library of madness once more. However, no such demands were immediately forthcoming, and so I passed my waking hours in a pathetic state of agitation.

The mere sight of any book was abhorrent to me, and only occasionally during my weary perambulations within the labyrinth of the abbey (whether these perambulations took me to some forgotten lumber-room or else to an abandoned bedchamber) did I accidentally come across a discarded and dusty volume. I shunned each such unwelcome discovery and left it untouched and unexamined, for the sight of ink befouling blank pages was, to me, akin to the sight of decay or disease festering its way over unblemished skin. Such was my bibliophobic mania that the thought of setting fire to the library itself crossed my mind repeatedly, a course of action—you will recall—I had recommended to the Revd. Winters as a surer remedy than his own proposal; namely, that of exorcism. On one occasion, I even went so far as to overcome my terror at the thought of entering into that hideous library, and attempted to gain access, taking with me a box of matches by which I could instigate a final conflagration of its entire, degenerate contents; but the heavy oaken door was locked and no amount of physical exertion on my part could make it yield. And from within I swore I could just make out the low chuckling of some revenant lector, who expressed wry amusement, mingled with contempt, at my clumsy attempts to force an entry.

During my crab-like perambulations throughout the endless maze of corridors, passageways, staircases, chambers, and halls that constituted the interior of Thool Abbey, I learnt that all other doors remained open to me—or, at least, those I encountered remained open to me. The structure was infinitely more spacious in its interior dimensions than I had hitherto imagined; a titanic space of enclosed immensity, subdivided into innumerable warrens and vaults. To chart the entirety of its confines in detail would surely have required months of labour. I confess that the sight alone of its modestly proportioned, mediaeval exterior would not have generated the anticipation of its stupendous internal grandeur; one on a sublime scale that only the awesome Gothic cathedrals of Europe could match, with the sole exception, perhaps, of that doomed, extravagant tribute to architectural phantasmagoria which the author Beckford had caused to be erected at Fonthill in Wiltshire.

It was a matter of acute curiosity to me whither the denizens of Thool Abbey habitually disported themselves, for none of the chambers I had visited (save for my own) showed any traces of recent occupancy. Indeed, all appeared long abandoned and wholly given over to dust, cobwebs, and decay. I further recalled that shortly after my arrival at the abbey (was it really, as the Revd. Winters had claimed, eight years ago?) I had entertained concerns about blundering into Lady Degabaston's boudoir by accident, and the incongruity between such delicate notions and the grim reality of this spectre-cursed haunt now struck me as laughable.

Nevertheless, day after day, food and drink were left outside my attic room door—presumably put there by the elusive bony myrmidon during those intervals when I slept. My routine became one of repeated wanderings throughout the inexhaustible confines of the abbey's interior, with my cane supporting my enfeebled frame. I have hinted once before that it seemed to me its structure was not consistent in its topography; that, in the innermost depths, corridors and stairways appeared and disappeared, or else changed their size and shape, and it was hazardous to reply upon one's memory alone in order to find one's way back. On an occasion early on in my expeditions, I found myself in serious peril of losing my way in the shifting labyrinth, quite unable to retrace my steps, and with the sole candle I had brought with me upon the verge of guttering out; the wick having burnt down almost to the base. To have been marooned in the oppressive darkness of those internal passageways, like some beast lost in the subterranean recesses of an immense cave-system, would have been a fate too dreadful to contemplate.

Thereafter, I was careful to carry with me a plentiful supply of spare candles and matches in the pockets of my jacket, and I made personalised chalk-marks upon the stone walls of the most ancient parts and upon the timber beams or panelling of those portions which dated to a later period in history. It was these individual chalk-marks I made to assist my navigation which confirmed my supposition about the fluid nature of the internal structure of Thool Abbey. I often found them located in places I was certain I had not passed by in my outward journey; and yet, there the exact same chalk-marks were, in seemingly different places, upon the return leg of it.

After weeks of such exploratory endeavours (you will readily appreciate, however, that, as always, my calculations concerning the passage of time are provisional) there grew upon me the conviction that the reason I had not discovered any of the chambers wherein the denizens of the abbey habitually kept themselves was not a matter of their being incorporeal spirits (God knows I had witnessed enough to confirm the physical nature of their existence!), but rather that the internal arrangement of the abbey had altered itself precisely to divert me away from finding their haunts. It was obvious that the members of a witch-cult must gather together somewhere, not least for the undertaking of their blasphemous ceremonies and rites, and even if they did so outside in the woodlands, then there would be places within the abbey to which they would repair after such activities. At the very least they would dine together, though what kind of hideous feasts sustained them remained a matter of hideous conjecture. Surely, they could not persist upon my blood alone? Such a limited quantity would not be sufficient sustenance. They had made no recent attempt to apply leeches to my body, though I had noted at the time the ardent satisfaction they seemed to derive via some occult process of loathsome affiliation as their bloodsuckers had feasted upon me.

And then I determined upon a plan. I would transfer myself from my attic room and relocate to another chamber deeper within the central, mediaeval portion of the abbey. I would do so upon my next foray and not return to the Jacobean annexe, but bed down instead at random in some abandoned quarter. Were I to begin from a different point of origin it might be possible for me to temporarily thwart the constant alterations in the structure that were undertaken specifically to throw me off the scent. After all, they had hitherto known the starting point on each of my previous attempts. By the time my ruse was discovered and allowances made by them for it, I would already have gained an advantage, provided I acted swiftly . . .

So it was I found myself ensconced in a long-abandoned monk's cell deep within the mediaeval bulk of the abbey. I had not chosen the place in advance, for there was little chance that, having done so, I could have successfully redirected my steps to its location, and my discovery of it was the result of pure serendipity. I had already steeled myself to occupy one of the many dismal lumber rooms I have previously mentioned, and although it could not be said that the former monk's cell offered a comfortable berth, it was nevertheless tolerable. Of furnishings there were only a scant number; and these chiefly consisted of a low bed-frame riddled with woodworm and a three-legged stool. The presence of a narrow window, tapering to a peak, situated high up in one wall, at first confused me because I could not see how it could possibly open up to the outside world: the cell itself was located too far from any of Thool Abbey's exterior walls to allow for that possibility. But upon further examination, once I had used the stool to raise myself up to its level, I discovered that beyond its mullioned panes of lurid stained-glass was yet another corridor, one with an arched ceiling and of stunted dimensions, but whose actual extent my candlelight was powerless to reveal fully. It might have extended for no more than thirty feet, or it might have reached to infinity.

I had brought with me in a small trunk a further supply of tapers, two candlesticks, non-perishable foodstuffs, and water—enough to last for a few days (or "days" such as I had come to reckon them). And so I made myself as comfortable as I could, using some moth-eaten tapestry of faded design as my bedding. I had removed my jacket and whiled away the time by staring fixedly at the flickering light of a solitary taper I had lit, its jaundiced flame hemmed in on every side by the oppressive gloom.

All around me, but appearing to come from very far-off rather than close at hand, I heard the creaking and shifting of walls, chambers, and passageways, as if the abbey were furtively rearranging its own internal structure yet again, contorting itself into a mystifying shape.

In my pitiable state of isolation and dread, I was subject to a spate of further horrible imaginings and sometimes even thought myself, like the abbey, to be inhuman; for did I not carry within me a veritable library of contradictory thoughts, dreams, and visions, all of them contending against one another and clamouring for expression? I then considered my newly acquired terror of books; I, who had devoted my entire life to their cataloguing and appraisal! I, who was so conscious my intellectual powers reposed upon the study of volumes which had passed through my hands and then, for one reason or another—but, above all, the dictates of sheer poverty—had subsequently been lost to me! Is it not a monstrous confession to make if I declare that, in the past, the loss of certain cherished books has caused me, in the long run, as many—*if not more*—pangs and pains than the loss of flesh-and-blood lovers and friends, also long since departed?

If only it were the case that my memory proved infallible!—that, having once perused a volume, I could then conjure up in my mind all its myriad details! And yet, would perfect recollection in and of itself be sufficient? For how many times in my youth have I turned from a particular book with a sense of boredom or disgust, only to pick up the same volume years later and discover it held a genuine fascination which had previously been beyond my powers to discern? Is it not also the case that a studious hermit possessed of an extensive library, one who has withdrawn from the widest social circle of even the most brilliant associates, must enter upon a world of insight far greater in scope than that of the merely contemporary mind? It would be a world of ideas and dreams that the test of time itself has sifted and refined, a world not subject to the vicissitudes of intellectual and cultural fashion. Moreover, is not all so-called "progress" simply a disease that infects tradition, rotting it away from the inside? And yet . . . again, and yet! This is surely only yet another inhuman doctrine to hold.

I continued to stare at the flickering light of the taper I had lit, watching the wick slowly burn down, the sounds of the groaning reconstitution of Thool Abbey reminding me much of the thunder that had accompanied the terrifying dream of the charred Lilith Blake, dead but still dreaming, and resting deep within her tomb.

At some point the candle had burnt out, but before that event occurred I had drifted off into slumber. Exhaustion had been a constant companion, as my physical form had become enfeebled by confinement within Thool Abbey. When I did awake (after such an interval as I could not determine) I realised I had been spared entirely the further horror of freshly formed nightmares whilst sleeping in this unfamiliar quarter; either that or else my recollection refused to bring them to mind as I returned to full consciousness, leaving them mercifully lost within the fathomless depths of sleep. Momentarily, I even entertained the notion that this portion of the abbey lay just beyond the rim of the witch-cult's malefic telepathy and I was therefore outside their influence; but I quickly dismissed this pernicious notion. It could not be denied that I had actually gone deeper into the heart of their nexus rather than farther away from it; indeed, it had been my prime goal to achieve that selfsame aim. There might, however, have been some relaxation in their specific campaign against me, perhaps whilst they were engaged upon another sorcerous task demanding their full attention. At best I had succeeded perhaps only temporarily in evading them through having quit my attic room in the Jacobean annexe and relocating myself here.

The grinding sound of the structure furtively rearranging it-

self had also ceased, and now silence jointly reigned with darkness. I lay there immobile upon the low, wormy bedstead,
wrapped in the faded tapestry that served as both blanket and
mattress, until the creeping misery of my situation compelled
me to rise. My jacket was not to hand. I fumbled about in the
impenetrable gloom for means by which I might light one of
my plentiful supply of tapers in the room and, as my searching
fingers made contact with a matchbox, they rattled its contents. The noise was stark; amplified by the absence of all other
sound. It was only when I lit the candle, after striking a match,
that I then heard something moving beyond the narrow
stained-glass casement high up in the far wall.

I got to my feet and put on the jacket which had lain crumpled upon the floor.

That the presence was still some distance away seemed certain, for its faint, dragging movements were discernible only
with the closest attention on my part; and whether it had been
summoned by the noise I had made or by the light from my taper, I could not say. I thought of extinguishing the wick, for
although it might be drawn hither by the illumination, perhaps
light itself was abhorrent to such a creature spawned of darkness. If so, then the thing had already detected the dim glow
that must have filtered through that small peaked window
above me. In any case, I had no desire to encounter the intrud-
er in total darkness.

My ears strained to catch every cadence of its laboured approach towards the monk's cell. There were even times when it
paused, as if through indecisiveness, but eventually the dragging sound persisted, becoming more and more definite as I
listened, with sweat now pouring from my brow. At one juncture I leapt for the door, seeking to flee along the passageway
outside: I found it immovable, though I pulled at its handle and

beat at its panelling with my gloved hands—employing all the limited strength that was mine to command. Feeble, futile attempts to jar it from its frame with my shoulder only seemed to encourage the efforts of the thing to redouble its inexorable, torturous advance.

At last, the culmination of the terror was achieved. The sound of that abominable thing dragging itself along the hunched corridor beyond the window gave way to the noise of it actually pawing at the wall that divided us in order to haul itself up to the aperture and to gain admittance via the casement.

As I stood there, with my back to the traitorous door, holding aloft the taper in front of me in the desperate hope that ever-closer proximity to light might ward it off rather than serve as a beacon to the thing, I saw through the flickering shadows (for my uncertain grasp upon the candlestick was as one afflicted by palsy) the casement slowly open towards me and two deathly white hands—each of them with long fingers like the spindly legs of some enormous spider—crawl over and grip the window ledge. Once the limbs had gained the necessary traction, there then appeared within the aperture a face, with most of its features charred or burnt away, yet still bearing blank, repugnant, unblinking eyes, a framing mass of raven-black hair, and a death's-head smile with sharp, yellow, needle-like teeth; half a face only, but one, of course, I knew only too well from the depths of nightmare—that of the hideous Lilith Blake. And, instantly, I was put in mind of the sight of a waxing moon rising above the horizon at night.

The thing had wedged itself into its lofty place, and I wondered whether the apparition might be capable of alteration in its bodily form so as to squeeze through an aperture that was far too small to allow the admittance of any fully grown person. Having gained and settled in its current position it then endeavoured to do so, and its form took on a momentarily fluid nature, the torso and hips narrowing as it forced its way into the monk's cell, before crawling face down along the wall and coming to rest at the base. It lay there, like some infernal bleached python, and stared up at me with those blank, black-rimmed, repugnant eyes. Then, even more shockingly, it actually began to laugh: there was to be no repetition of the siren-call I had heard when previously drawn down in a dream to Blake's book-lined crypt.

The laughter was high and musical, laced with contempt, a laughter directed at those who, myself included, were numbered amongst the living, and it evinced unparalleled self-pleasure in its own supremacy, at its having trampled down and conquered over life itself. It was the deathless joy of total negation given voice. To listen to it any further would be to yield to—no, *to cherish forever* the grave rather than the womb.

I could scarcely think, let alone stand upright: such was the degree of the terror that coursed through my frame; but, mustering my last reserves of courage, I took up my walking cane and prepared to bring it down repeatedly upon Lilith Blake's skull until I had silenced that mocking laughter. In some dim recess of my rational mind I knew this pathetic attempt at defiance would be futile.

And just as I had pulled back my arm to strike a first blow the laughter ceased, and the revenant's belly was bloodlessly split asunder from within; there appeared a gaping rent upon the front of her dusty shroud, one which rapidly widened of its own accord, splitting the funereal garment into two separate parts, and what was revealed inside was the dead hollow of her womb and an open book therein. It was a volume of crumpled black leather with pages of vellum which were then rifled back and forth by the revenant's long, delicate, and spider-like pair of white hands until a certain point in the text was reached.

I lowered my walking cane to my side and thrust forward the candlestick I carried in my other hand, advancing haltingly closer towards the macabre sight of that creature lying upon the floor, my fear kept in check by the irresistible demands of my own curiosity. I resolved to glimpse what lay behind these manifestations of nightmarishness: the even more fantastical secrets beyond the outward forms of Thool Abbey's degenerate actors and behind the garish scenery of its *grand guignol*. Here, it seemed, was the very script which directed the entire ghastly performance.

But, of course, I can speak only figuratively, with my thoughts twisted into metaphors, and cannot express the ulti-mate meaning of the incomprehensible gibberish I saw printed upon the pages of the volume snugly nestled within Lilith Blake's desiccated womb. Certainly I had already expected to see it was not a printed book, but rather one that was hand-written, and I had already thought it would be impossible to comprehend; for was it not vouchsafed to me in dreams that this tome did not consist of accounts of supernatural phenom-ena, but consisted of supernatural phenomena in themselves? Such may have been the case, and it is true I glimpsed only a few words that fixed themselves in my rapidly disordered con-sciousness (synonyms of "terror," "fear," "hands," "shadow," "night," "darkness," and "dead"), but what caused me to actual-ly snuff out the taper, so I might see no more of the incoherent revelation that had been revealed to me, was simply this: the contents of that passage had not been penned by the evil white hands of Lilith Blake, for the penmanship undeniably marked it out as a product of my own handiwork. It was an even more deranged continuation of that "bibliography" over which I had laboured whilst trapped in the library of madness.

# Chapter Ten

Why then was this forbid? Why but to awe,
Why but to keep ye low and ignorant,
His worshipper; he knows that in the day
Ye eat thereof, your eyes that seem so clear,
Yet are but dim, shall perfectly be then
Opened and cleared, and ye shall be as gods,
Knowing both good and evil as they know.
—JOHN MILTON, *Paradise Lost,* Book IX

During the ensuing frenzied delirium caused by those revelations I must have extricated myself from the confines of the monk's cell and the presence of Lilith Blake; for when I eventually regained my senses, I found myself in a distant alcove in another part of the abbey, now footsore, bruised, and gasping for air, with my cane resting across my legs. I can offer no account of how I came to be elsewhere, for I had lost my reason from the moment I had snuffed out the candle. The intervening period is simply a series of confused, backward impressions in which I plunged along passageways of utter darkness, not caring where I was bound, being concerned solely to increase as much as possible the distance between myself and the monstrosity I had seen by candlelight. That it was I who had penned those words in the book seemed impossible to deny, and yet I had no memory at all of having done so, and even though the extent of what I had glimpsed had been mercifully brief, still I had seen enough of what had been written down there to convince me I had delineated an innermost hell. And if I had written the words unknowingly, who, then, had dictated their final form if not Lilith Blake? Did I not already suspect that the creation of the book whose title was *The White Hands* was not the sum total of the machinations of the witch-cult, but rather that, after the text was loosed upon the world, its privations would continue to spread and manifest themselves in ever more hideous, ever more unimaginable, forms of polymorphous corruption?

All I could do was attempt to make my way to another part of the abbey, perhaps even to retreat in defeat to my old attic room. I had to acknowledge to myself that my endeavours to discover the secret hiding place of its denizens had been a dismal failure. Wherever I turned in this gaunt, grim labyrinth, no solutions were forthcoming; and what was revealed to me were the further labyrinths that lurked within; for is not a book a labyrinth and is not thought a maze—twists and turnings determined solely by an arrangement of words in a particular order? And might not Thool Abbey, like the universe itself, harbour some secret language of its own, some arrangement or pattern, though not of words, nor even mathematical equations or musical notation, but one whose symbols are literally indecipherable by us?

I hastily went through the pockets of my jacket-coat and was relieved to find in them my small reserve supply of emergency matches and candles. I had no candle holder, however, and so was forced to clutch one of the lit tapers in my left hand (my cane was in the right); the kid-gloves I wore in memory of the Revd. Winters protected me from the stinging blobs of hot, dribbling wax.

I did not know how long it had been since I had last taken water, but the period must have been lengthy, for my throat and mouth were parched. I tramped along the pitch-dark corridors once more, and there was still no trace of the chalk-

marks that would have assisted me in my homeward navigation. I was as cursed as Maturin's Melmoth or Coleridge's Ancient Mariner, though cursed not to range ceaselessly across
the globe as they had been—but rather to wander in an infinity
reduced to a cryptic series of chambers, halls, and corridors.

No ominous sound did Thool Abbey make: there came to
my ears no creaking of timber, no grinding of stone against
stone. I supposed the structure was in a quiescent phase, and
the magical powers of the witch-cult that could transform the
interior were being temporarily held in abeyance. Nevertheless,
I found myself passing along a multitude of warped passageways, askew galleries, and off-centre winding staircases that be-
tokened very recent, yet not quite coherent, radical alterations.

I discovered a second turret—one whose existence I had
not suspected and which had certainly not been visible when
last (how long ago!) I had seen the abbey exterior. Had this
second turret also been thrown up like some monstrous new
appendage by the structure's occult system of reorganisation?
Was it yet another attempt to throw me off the track? I could
not answer such a question without further evidence, and so I
laboriously scaled its corkscrew stairwell, the steps narrow,
treacherous, and coated with omnipresent red lichen, my dizzying ascent made all the more perilous by the nebulous cobwebs and the increasingly mephitic air. The foulness of the
latter even threatened, on occasion, to extinguish my feeble
candle-flame. It was surely the exhalation of a mustiness from
an antique chamber which had been shut up for centuries.

Finally I achieved the uppermost level of the turret after an
interminable climb and rested at the arched entranceway to a
chamber housed underneath the pinnacle of the roof. Gasping
both from the exertion and the debilitating effect of the poi-
sonous air, I leant upon my walking cane and gazed steadily at

the low, crooked, worm-eaten door that stood before me. There was no lock, and by pushing my weight against the portal I managed to shift it open inwards just wide enough to allow me to pass through. Thus it was that, candle aloft, I began to explore the greater mysteries of the upper region and entered into the infernal heaven of the witch-cult.

I knew now why the musty stench was so suffocating. The turret chamber was windowless, with no means for the air to circulate except via the stairwell. The red lichen had penetrated directly into its confines. Only the light from my own taper penetrated the gloom. I wished to make a thorough examination of the numerous objects I could see radiating inwards from the circular wall of the chamber, but my initial impression consisted of a series of oblong objects resembling funeral caskets. Directly above my head, at the apex of the timbers that supported the turret roof, there hung a large, iron-wrought candelabrum with a pulley mechanism attached to it and whose descent and ascent was operated by an attached length of rope. The end of this rope I found fixed around a metal ring set into one of the flagstones underfoot; with little difficulty I soon managed to lower the candelabrum down to chest-height. Using my own candle-flame, I lit the other tapers and then raised the device back up into its lofty perch below the peaked ceiling.

With the shadows now forced into the extreme reaches of the chamber, I saw that my first impression had been accurate: the oblong boxes did indeed resemble coffins, at least in shape and size, but in fact they were actually a dozen or so wooden crates—formed of planks of wood that had been nailed together—which the red lichen had seized in its pestilential embrace. They were arranged all along the circumference of the wall, and above each one of them there hung a framed portrait rendered in oil-colours. Between the paintings hung a series of individual draperies, bearing upon their tapestried surfaces what appeared to be grotesque mandalas of some cryptic, unearthly design. I did not immediately take the opportunity to examine these portraits and banners in all their details, for they were far back in the shadows and my wild-eyed, roving attention was taken up by two other objects that were closer at hand. One was an open trunk stuffed with papers, whilst the other was what appeared to be a surgeon's operating table surrounded by all manner of outré paraphernalia that was not connected with the medical profession, as I might have supposed, but rather with some artistic pursuit such as modelling.

However, it was to the mysterious trunk which I first repaired (although I did not linger long over its contents: the sight of all writing was still abhorrent to me). Glancing through a small sample of the vast number of papers therein, I found it contained correspondence received by Dr Cressop from various agencies or actors who were involved in malefic plots and formed a central archive of their activities. The dates were wildly incongruous, indicating an existence of impossible longevity on the part of the recipient, and three examples alone, which I shall outline here from memory, will suffice to demonstrate their variety.

One was from the War Office and dated to 1939, being a telegram querying the complete disappearance of representatives who had been sent to Thool Abbey in order to secure its legal requisition under the War Powers Emergency Act of His Majesty George VI's Government. The next dated to 1752, hailed from both Sir Francis Dashwood and John Montagu, Fourth Earl of Sandwich, witnessing their joint desire to associate a newly-established occult order, "The 'Monks' of Medmenham," with the earlier occult order which already obtained at Thool Abbey. The last was a series of conspiratorial communications in French that appeared to date from the turn of this century, from *La Société des Âmes Mortes* in Paris.

Had I possessed the willpower and inclination to examine in depth the contents of that trunk, I have little doubt they would have amply confirmed the Revd. Alphonsus Winters's contention that the Thool witch-cult radiated tentacles of spiritual contagion down the centuries and across the whole of Europe and beyond.

But by then my attention was diverted to the apparent "surgeon's table" with its surrounding array of instruments, sealed vats, and tins holding chemical agents, as well as metal chests containing large quantities of sheets of paper-pulp with text and certain framing cryptograms already infused upon their surfaces. Upon closer inspection of these materials I realised all were employed in the production of life-sized papier-mâché models. This was, then, Dr Cressop's very own "workshop of filthy creation." Were his visitations to the library of madness far below occasions used to select and then to ferry up into the heights of the turret-tower certain blasphemous texts required by him as raw material for his creations? Did the red-lichen-coated series of crates that radiated from the walls of the turret chamber not house the dead bodies of the Degabaston line and of their favoured confederates in the witch-cult, but rather house cadaverous simulacra? But how, then, to account for the portrait paintings hung in turn above each of these oblong boxes? Was it from these pictorial representations that Cressop had refined his own labours, refashioning the papier-mâché outlines into duplicate forms? I had not yet examined these artworks at close quarters, and now did so, carrying my taper over to the nearest one at hand.

It was a painting of a young woman whose features I felt to be familiar to me in some indefinable manner and whose aspect was of the most striking. The execution of the portrait was masterly. The naturalistic brushstrokes and keen attention to subtleties of light and shade were almost photographic in their fidelity to lifelikeness. The subject, despite her youthfulness, had an imperious expression and her piercing cobalt-coloured eyes glared across the gulf of centuries between us. The spectral effect of those eyes was only accentuated by the fact that, again, despite her youthfulness, her luxuriant hair was completely white, with not a blemish of any other colour. This hair she wore kept up, in that style I supposed was *de rigueur* at the time. The antique design of the high-necked dress, in funereal, mourning black, dated it to the Victorian era. In her imperious expression there lurked a suggestion of contempt (particularly in the cruel line of her mouth), and it was this pernicious element alone which mitigated against the natural beauty that might otherwise have made her the object of some abject lover's adoration. Was this Lilith Blake before flames had disfigured her features into a twisted caricature? The hands, of course, would have told the tale; but the hands of the young woman in this portrait were not those of Lilith Blake. Although one could not deny the fingers were of an unusual length, they were not possessed of the same degree of macabre bizarrerie.

I tried to shake off the impression that the sight of her features held for me more than a commonplace sense of *déjà vu*, and had I not myself been deprived of sight of a mirror for a period longer than I could reckon, perhaps then certain familial lineaments would have been brought into sharper relief. As it was, my thoughts returned to the mystery concerning the identity of the portrait's subject.

This was partially dispelled when I noticed a date of 1860

had been appended to one corner of the canvas. That datum clearly indicated it had been completed fourteen years before Lilith Blake's birth, so it was not her depicted on the canvas. And when my gaze dropped from the painting to the lid of the red-lichen-mottled crate that rested directly beneath it, the mystery was fully dispelled; for I saw a brass plate bearing the name "Lady Caroline Degabaston."

So Isis was unveiled at last! My thoughts lingered momentarily over the reasons for her wearing a veil in later life—surely not through vanity? It was certain the abnormal longevity of her lifespan would have wreaked unavoidable physical depredations upon a face once possessed of beauty in youth. Might it not be that she went veiled solely in my presence, and in order to conceal from me personally some suggestive association which only I might fully apprehend?

The lid of the crate was easily removed, and I was glad of the gloves that prevented skin contact with the red-lichen-smeared across the wooden surface. I feared contamination by touching that vile organism, an organism which seemed to play some rôle, as yet unaccountable, in linking together facets of the horrors within Thool Abbey.

I have previously used the term "an infernal heaven" to describe the turret-tower, so let me not neglect to give due attention in turn to the abnormal occupants of that lofty chamber.

What lurked within the crate, the thing I saw by candlelight, was precisely what I anticipated would be contained there: a monstrous papier-mâché dummy, one presumably fashioned by the peculiar methods Dr Cressop employed. The resemblance to the person of Lady Caroline was outwardly only superficial, for the nature of his raw materials did not facilitate an authentic likeness. Still, he had gone so far as to clothe the thing in the oblong box with raiment presumably worn in life by its human model, had fitted it with a wig of long white hair, and had also inserted a pair of glass eyes with cobalt-coloured, grey-blue irises.

If I call the appearance of that dummy wildly grotesque, I do not do it an injustice. I was appalled by the chief character-istic of the thing; for it had been formed from strips of chemi-cally treated, transparent pulp-paper bearing writings and framing cryptograms. And the latter mirrored the designs upon the banners which had been draped alongside the portraits— the same designs which I have already termed grotesque man-dalas in an attempt to convey their utterly unearthly nature.

Of the writings themselves and what information they con-tained, I must state that I recognised certain passages which had been torn out in strips from the most barbarous of the vol-umes housed in the library of madness, passages that were supposedly possessed of a certain power in and of themselves, passages which, once seen, do not leave the mind of the reader but linger there indefinitely and which adopt a parasitic exist-ence in an individual's consciousness.

My gaze scanned the dimly lit recesses of the turret-tower, taking in the radiating circle of crates, the mandala-riddled banners and the other shadowy portraits which hung beside them. Doubtless those crates also contained grotesque doppel-gängers formed to represent others of the Degabaston line as well as their most favoured confederates.

Might it not be the case that these dummies were akin to magical, life-sized effigies, infused with occult power by the texts and cryptograms which comprised the substance of their bodies, a veritable labyrinth of cross-referenced and interrelat-ed diabolic spells arranged in a unique order? If so, did they then confer upon their original models not perpetual youth, but the final suspension of death and decomposition? Might the continued existence of these effigies, these idols of god-like self-worship, hidden high up in an infernal heaven, prolong obscenely the existence of the real physical forms of the Degabastons and their close confederates, even at the cost of their immortal souls? *Would they age indefinitely but never die?* To what extent did they then retain their own minds or own power of volition and not become, in reality, a hideous compound? Were their identities compromised by some greater, controlling portion, an invading fragment of an unspeakable force outside space and time which now subtly directed their actions and their thoughts? Did this force also manifest itself in certain telltale physical aberrations when it was resident within human forms, aberrations such as a profoundly disturbing asymmetry of facial features, spider-like white hands of extraordinary length, and the extreme prolongation of the lifespan of any offspring? And did it, furthermore, permeate into one's dreams so that even sleep proved to be no refuge?

Just when did the unspeakable force first gain hold over the accused line of Degabaston? The Revd. Winters had stated the corruption had first set in during the sixteenth century with Charles, the Sixth Baron. But surely he had only prefigured the full flourishing of evil by dabbling in it, and had merely set the scene with his puerile contempt for all religion and enthusiasm for Machiavellian intrigues. No, it was his son, the nameless Seventh Baron, of whom historical traces are not extant, who was the missing link in the whole chain, and who had subsequently taken full command of the stage. Francis, First Earl of Thool, son of this Seventh Baron, though himself a supreme master of wickedness, had merely consolidated the nexus of the witch-cult.

I closed the lid of the crate containing the effigy of Lady Caroline and began to examine, in turn, the other portraits hung upon the circular wall of that "infernal heaven." What a motley chamber of horrors was there displayed! Here was depicted in oil-colours that fiend whom I had seen once before: Gerald, Second Earl of Thool, who married an idiot bride, his face leering down at me with the aristocratic scorn and the piercing eyes that were prevalent in the familial lineaments of all the Degabastons. I did not dwell long upon that fixed glare. Beside him lurked the bony myrmidon, with his lopsided features and bloodshot left-eye. This portrait was executed in a less well-executed style (one befitting his lowly station) than that of Lord Gerald, but it nevertheless captured the sardonic yet obsequious aura which I had come to loathe in the servant's demeanour. Several other portraits remained for me to examine, but upon reaching the next proximate one, the effect upon me was so terrible I felt stunned into disbelief at the evidence of my eyes.

I raised my candle all the closer to this third portrait in the hope that light would dispel the dread impression which had shaken me to the core. Rather than dispelling the impression, its accuracy was hideously confirmed, and there could be no room for doubt in the matter.

There, in the third portrait, my own features stared back at me. And yet, there was in those features some subtle deviation that could not be accounted for in a physical sense: the deviation could only be explained if the central mind which directed that double was possessed of a deep-seated malice. Such a trait I did not recognise as forming a motivating power in my personality; but that it had also been present in the features of Lady Caroline Degabaston was impossible to gainsay.

This double of mine depicted in the third portrait was garbed in the extravagant fashion of the seventeenth century, with the outward appearance of having been a Royalist cavalier during the English Civil War. He, too, leant upon a cane for support, and I supposed it the result of a wound he had received in that conflict. Desperately I sought in vain for some telltale sign the painting was a fake and had actually been produced in the modern era, but evidence of a delicate, web-like series of almost imperceptible cracks that covered the surface, as well as a patina of antiquity, refuted such a proposition entirely.

Still reeling at the tremendous shock I had experienced, my thoughts nevertheless turned to the crate that lay directly beneath the portrait; for each of them bore a nameplate which indicated the identity both of its "occupant" and of the person depicted in the accompanying painting. And the wording on that particular nameplate was enough to make me speculate again upon the true extent to which my actions were directed by my own will or were directed by the will of an outside force:

SAUL, SEVENTH BARON DE GABASTON

"Saul"—even my Christian name! Whence, then, had my surname "Prior" derived? Was it, like Blake's own surname, some appellation foisted upon a supposedly orphaned infant so as to mask its true ancestral heritage? Or was the choice of "Prior" a mocking play upon words made at my expense? Had my existence up until my arrival at Thool Abbey been nothing but a series of carefully planned deceptions conceived by the witch-cult centuries before I was even born? Had false memories been subsequently implanted into my mind by diabolism?

But I had not plumbed the fullest depths of the nightmarish mystery. I had hitherto opened only the crate containing the effigy of Lady Caroline Degabaston, being confident the other ones would merely harbour further examples of the abominations wrought by the foul wizardry of Dr Cressop. But what of

this crate which contained the effigy of Saul, the Seventh Baron—he who was the key not only to this enigmatic conspiracy
but also to the true nature of my own identity? What secret
was housed within this particular abyss?

I set down my candle and steeled myself to draw aside the
lid and to reveal what the mottled casket contained. Eventually
I summoned up the courage to do so, kneeling and by now
wholly oblivious to my surroundings.

What I saw laid out there within was the culmination of my
quest. The effigy was obviously only partially completed—
although fully dressed in the flamboyant apparel of the seventeenth century—and this doppelgänger possessed no head. I
loosened its clothing in order to see the torso of the incomplete
effigy, and found that it (like the effigy of Lady Caroline) was
formed of an interminable series of pasted strips of chemically
treated transparent paper covered with text and framing cryptograms. I confess that, at first sight of the writings, I expected
they would be yet another deranged continuation of the "bibliography" over which I had laboured whilst chained up in the
library of madness, but this was not so. With mocking irony,
the text that had been torn and rearranged in this embryonic
effigy of the Seventh Baron—or of me!—was an account of my
existence, but it was an account that had been continually re-
vised, altered and twisted like some eternal palimpsest of textual metempsychosis. Obviously, given the structure of the
effigy and the intertwining strips of paper upon which the information had been imparted, no more than fragments of my
supposed life were visible to me at any one moment, but even
in that warped totality there could be no doubt it was my existence which was being subjected to the machinations of the
witch-cult, and had been since the moment of my conception.
That I was myself of the Degabaston line could no longer be

denied. Nor could there remain any doubt it was Lilith Blake who had spawned me; writing me into existence like a living grimoire.

Two other features of this ghastly, partially formed effigy compounded the sickening horror with which I was ultimately confronted: the first was that motley red lichen which had extended its venomous contamination to proliferate in detestable, hairy patches in the hollowed-out neck cavity; the second was the formation of its hands, for they were the telltale white hands, those shaped like huge five-limbed spiders with attenuated fingers of inordinate length. Both of these hands, moreover, were blank, with no writing or cryptograms upon them.

The sight of these appendages inevitably made me wonder what physical changes might be being wrought upon me, and what prophecies might be being fulfilled in my person. I held my gloved hands up to the candlelight. Had the fingers, in fact, grown longer since I had first donned the gloves? Surely not, for, like the Revd. Winters's own hands, had not mine also always been of unusual delicacy and length?

I was not sure; I could not trust my memories, let alone trust my own judgement. But the thought of the fallen clergyman did bring to mind the solution I had earlier proposed to annihilate the horrors of the library of madness and which had not been put into effect by him. So I resolved to take that course of action here and now: to end it all with a purging by fire, the age-old remedy against witchcraft. The rotten contents of the turret-tower would go up in flames if I set a taper to the cryptic draperies, the portraits, and the papier-mâché doubles in their caskets. And, in such a mighty conflagration, the whole of Thool Abbey could not fail to be consumed by fire in turn. I prayed that if my life were to be forfeit as a result, the entirety of the Degabaston line might also be terminated.

"Ah, here you are, my Lord. You have certainly led us a merry dance."

It was the voice of Dr Cressop.

Such had been my state of distraction I had not been cognisant, until those words were uttered, of the fact a dozen forms had filed into the turret chamber with ghostly stealth, bearing with them a coffin with a glass-panelled lid.

It was as if the portraits had escaped to form a wizened, death's-head parade; the witch-cult had reconvened in their infernal heaven, prior to undertaking some new ceremony of diabolism.

And amidst the ghastly coven was the now-unveiled Lady Caroline Degabaston—she with skin covering a skeletal face that was no more than a loathsome mask of mottled red lichen; though her piercing, cobalt-coloured eyes were every bit as vivid and imperious as the eyes of her portrait-painting. For it was in the centuries-annihilating intensity of that gaze that the long reach of the tainted Degabaston lineage could be traced down through generation after generation, even unto me.

# Chapter Eleven

... the house of life was riven asunder and the human trinity dissolved, and the worm which never dies, that which lies sleeping within us all, was made tangible and an external thing, and clothed with a garment of flesh. And then, in the hour of midnight, the primal fall was repeated and re-presented, and the awful thing veiled in the mythos of the Tree in the Garden was done anew. Such was the *nuptiae Sabbati.*—ARTHUR MACHEN, *The Three Impostors*

I was held fast in the grip of the assembled coven and then dragged to the coffin they had carried with them into that infernal heaven. It had been only recently exhumed from the ground, judging by the clods of earth with which it was still partially caked. A look of telepathically shared satisfaction seemed to pass over the twisted faces of each member of the witch-cult as the window-panelled coffin lid was prised off by Dr Cressop. I had thought the casket might be empty and it was myself who was about to become its occupant; but in fact it contained a bloated corpse with a twisted neck, one dressed in the Royalist Cavalier garb of the seventeenth century, and with a livid yet horribly familiar countenance—Saul, Seventh Baron De Gabaston. Yet this was a relatively fresh dead body, one presumably hanged and not some unnatural corpse that had lain dead and dreaming for centuries, having staved off the effects of decomposition. How could this be? My searching gaze alighted on the hands of the dead Baron: they were the white hands, long, pale, and hideous; exact duplicates (or perhaps the original!) of those appendages which also graced the headless effigy housed in the crate beneath its portrait-painting.

Dr Cressop, assisted by the bony myrmidon, hauled the cadaver out of the coffin and onto the surgeon's table where, to my appalled disgust, they then began to behead the mortal remains with a bone-saw. This desecration was looked on with barely concealed enthusiasm by the other members of the coven, who still held me fast, forcing me to witness the whole ghoulish operation. The sound of their laboured breathing became louder, at first suffused with a rasping whisper, until finally they began to chant the unspeakable words of an incantatory rite.

With great ceremony and after much labour, Dr Cressop then bore aloft the decapitated head of the corpse of Saul, the Seventh Baron, and carried it to the crate beneath his portrait. He knelt down reverently and placed it upon the red-lichen-mottled neck-stump of the headless, papier-mâché effigy which lay there. He then stood up, made a curious sign of inverted benediction with his left hand over the composite abomination, and took a few paces backwards to observe his handiwork, tilting his head from side to side in a gesture of indefinable contemplation.

The chanting of the coven reached a frightful crescendo, seeming to seep into my brain and accentuating the terror which gripped me: for I felt certain that my—or was it Lord Saul's?—effigy-hybrid was now upon the brink of an unholy animation and would at any instant stiffly sit up in its crate, open wide its eyes, and turn an aeons-blasting cobalt-grey stare upon me. Surely a charnel resurrection by fusion of death with the embodied occult *logos* had been the purpose of the ceremony? And yet . . . three-hundred years. Suddenly the chanting ceased abruptly.

The culmination proved not to be bodily animation of my perverse doppelgänger, but the rapid creeping of the mottled red lichen upwards from the join at the base of the effigy's neck. It spread like a rapacious blight over the newly attached corpse-head of Lord Saul. Within a few minutes the lichen contaminated all the dead human flesh, transforming entirely its formerly livid hue into one of dappled crimson.

And at my elbow, the similarly incarnadined face of Lady Caroline Degabaston pressed close to my own, eyes blazing with the fire of inner devilry, and I smelt the foulness of her breath, lungs exhaling the perfume of indefinitely suspended decay.

Dr Cressop solemnly stepped forward, replaced the lid of the crate, and made a courteous bow. Then, with stately grace, he made his way to the surgeon's table where lay the now-headless corpse of Lord Saul. Was it my imagination alone or did I witness a slight, almost imperceptible tremor of anticipation pass through the otherwise rigid form of that headless corpse?

The doctor gestured to the coven to bring me to him and, despite my desperate efforts to free myself from their grasp, their superior numbers were more than sufficient to overpower me. I was myself surely now as aged as all those who sojourned too long within the confines of Thool Abbey.

"It is time again for me to administer a dose of the amber draft, which has too long been denied you, my Lord," he said. "Soon all worldly cares will fly from you and you will reawaken fully into that existence which is your birthright and is our continuum."

He prepared the soporific, dream-destroying solution whose contents were drawn from the familiar bottle bearing the sign of the skull-and-crossbones.

Again I thought I saw the headless body twitch upon the surgeon's table.

Some alien voice bubbled up within me, demanding its right of expression, uttering a question I myself had not formulated but whose significance I nevertheless recognised as imperative.

"The year?" I heard myself saying, croakily.

"It is now 1648 again, my Lord—the year of your first exhumation. We have turned the progress of the entire universe back upon its own track in the Great Ceremony: the past has been made anew and where it is necessary that some are written into existence, therefore others must be written out of it."

And then I willingly drank deeply, and temporary oblivion swiftly followed.

I awoke to find myself once more in my attic room, high up in the Jacobean annexe. My return to consciousness was a slow ascent up from the depths of drugged sleep, and at first I felt a sense of nausea and disorientation at the very prospect of wakefulness itself. Some noise was insistently calling me to reality, but it was a noise I fervently wished to ignore.

When at last I opened my eyes, I felt immense relief I was not still in the infernal heaven of that mysterious turret-tower and subject to the insane machinations of the witch-cult.

Candlelight had been provided for my benefit and the wicks had not burnt down, so I assumed the tapers had been lit not more than a few hours previously. Outside, in the depths of the woodlands, the teratological monsters were howling in chorus with a hitherto unsurpassed degree of baleful intensity. I now knew them to be all those accursed souls who had come to Thool Abbey—either as enemies or as potential, but failed, confederates of the witch-cult—and who were permitted to remain within its wider environs solely as tormented, mindless outcasts.

It was when I tried to sit up that I found my limbs were paralysed. I managed to lift my head forward so my chin touched my chest and saw my whole body below the neck was covered by a dusty funeral shroud. There were disturbing patches of yellow and red discolouration upon its fabric. Although I attempted over and over again to will my limbs to work, they were as lifeless as clay. I tried to cry out, but emitted only a gargling croak, and even this action sent spasms of pain along my throat. I felt a sensation as if I might choke to death upon my own saliva were I to continue to attempt to utter any sound, so instead I lay there silently, turning my head from side to side in impotent frustration, and could not blot out the inverted paean (to misery and eternal darkness) emanating from the woodlands.

Later Dr Cressop arrived and lit fresh candles to replace those which had by then guttered out. He explained that he wished to make an examination of my numb, inanimate body, pulling the shroud up over my head and preventing my having any view of proceedings. I saw, however, a pile of clothing—Royalist Cavalier garb—upon the adjacent chair. I was still almost incapable of speech, and whenever I attempted to communicate with him he cautioned me not to do so. When his examination was complete he then replaced the sheet in its original position. I noted, however, the Royalist garments were gone; replaced by the clothes I had myself formerly worn. He spoon-fed me a disgusting blood-red gruel from a bowl. I had not eaten, it seemed, for days, and such was my hunger that I fairly gulped down the foul-tasting muck. He complimented me on the return of my appetite and digestive powers, but advised me this was the last meal I would enjoy for some considerable time.

"Now, my Lord, you have to undertake the last journey necessary to bring you back to us in your entirety," he said. "As it
was before."

He departed the attic room but returned within the hour,
and with him were four of the more able-bodied members of
the witch-cult, carrying between them the same coffin with a
glass-windowed lid in which the corpse of Saul the Seventh
Baron had lain before his late disinterment. With the shroud
still covering my body below the neck, his entourage solemnly
lifted me from the bunk and deposited me in the red-silk-
cushioned casket, and then closed the lid. I saw what happened
next through the small window in the coffin lid, following
events with the tormented helplessness of one doubly lost in
nightmare and subject to sleep-paralysis.

With Dr Cressop at the head, bearing a candelabrum, they
carried the coffin down through the interminable passageways,
halls, and chambers of the abbey until, eventually, a funeral
cortège of all the remaining nobles and other confederates of
the witch-cult was assembled.

Outside, in the eternally night-haunted grounds, torches
were lit, and they began again the same chanting which had
accompanied the ritual of decapitation, with Lady Caroline
leading the incantation; she reading from that loathsome, ines-
capable book bound in crumpled black leather (whose crimson
text was penned by a hand whose stylistic idiosyncrasies were
very familiar to me).

The coffin was slowly ferried up the carriage driveway. I
heard the crunching footfalls of the cortège upon its gravel
path, while my gaze was fixed upon the deadly-black starless
sky above, and my useless body jarred and shifted with the
stumbling advance of the casket bearers. On and on went the
chanting, though I overheard certain queries and answers be-

ing exchanged between Dr Cressop, Lord Gerald, and the bony myrmidon.

"The way is clear, you're certain?"

"All is in readiness."

"The villagers?"

"Dead. Murdered in their beds."

"We must not be seen—even by a wayward traveller not of this locality."

"Ha! I should pity such an unfortunate! Eyes and tongue plucked out!"

"And the same grave? Know you well how vital this be to success?"

"Aye, the very same plot, in unconsecrated ground, where they sought first to keep him from us!"

"All is in readiness, I swear, by my troth."

By the glare of the flaming torches held aloft by the cortège, I saw we had reached those twin pillars where perched the red-lichen-mottled stone gargoyles marking the limit of the estate. I knew we were now about to quit the occult environs of Thool Abbey. What could I expect to see upon gaining the outside world once more? Nausea and unconsciousness as before? Sunlight? Surely not the latter; for these creatures of night could not hope to exist anywhere except in darkness, and it seemed the hour of this sojourn or excursion had been carefully calculated in advance.

I struggled to effect some movement of my limbs, hoping against hope the paralysis might have worn off and chance would allow me to attempt an escape the moment I was carried over the threshold. I thought of sunlit green fields and a beautiful clear blue sky, but when we finally crossed into the outer world it was merely a transition from night to night; both as apparently black and void-like as the other.

Nevertheless, that I was now in the outer world was certain. For as we advanced up over the steep hillside towards the outskirts of Gallows Langley, I could hear the hooting of an owl in the distance—a far-off, furtive sound but one absurdly welcome to me. It was the first bird-call I had heard since my imprisonment in that realm of the eternally dead. And, unless I were mistaken, some measure of control over my limbs had returned; for I felt an involuntary tremor course through my left leg, followed by the slight flicker of motion—which I had myself willed—in the fingers of my right hand! Hope surged up in my breast. Now I was finally outside Thool Abbey and its grounds, perhaps the power of the witch-cult no longer enjoyed mastery and I might yet flee from its terrible dominion.

If only they had ceased their infernal chanting!—for I was convinced that its baleful influence upon my brain was one of the primary factors in stultifying my own gradually returning powers of volition.

Ahead, at the brow of the hill, I saw a waxing crescent moon rising. It crept slowly into sight, like some sickly-yellow, horned beacon to which the witch-cult was being inexorably drawn. They had cast aside their now-fading torches, but still their maddening chant went on.

After half an hour or so more of the trek (how much easier did it seem for me to gauge the passage of time!) we reached the summit of the hill, passed over it, and then descended swiftly into a desolate valley—a blasted, ghastly, and treeless region; and at its heart there nestled a shunned burial-ground. Herein the self-outcast and the wilfully damned had been namelessly interred, their memory to be blotted out as a consequence of the hideous campaign against life itself which they had so eagerly waged through their practice of the blackest of all black sorceries.

The chanting finally ceased.

The witch-cult laid down the coffin on the ground, but I felt able at last to actually try and push up against the lid and attempt to free myself. Perhaps the element of surprise would gain me some small advantage. But curling tentacles of low ground-mist washed over the glass window-panel of the coffin and I saw, through the haze, the lichen-mottled crimson face of Lady Caroline gaze at me with a knowing leer. I managed only to lever the lid up by a few inches and then, through the aperture I had myself created, the loathsome book was deposited inside the coffin with me. At a signal from Lady Caroline, the bony myrmidon rapidly nailed down the lid whilst the weight of the others held it secure. I saw Dr Cressop take Lady Caroline's place, his wizened face peering through the window-panel with a look of satanic satisfaction. He made that curious left-handed sign of inverted benediction over my casket; then, with myself still trapped within, the witch-cult lowered it back into the recently reopened grave whence Lord Saul himself had lately been disinterred.

I now knew what was to be my ultimate fate; and the price of my release from Thool Abbey was that of my being buried alive. I had merely exchanged darkness for a deeper darkness, terror for a greater terror, one prison for another; an insanely vast labyrinth for a narrow house.

Soil began raining down upon the coffin; it was not long before the window-panel was blocked entirely and I could see nothing more. However, I still heard the clods of earth splattering upon the lid until, in a short while, it was covered over, and all outside noise became deadened as the grave was slowly filled in completely. Finally the silence was broken solely by the sound of my own hollow breathing and the curiously arrhythmic but slow beating of my heart.

Death did not curtail my existence. Over the course of the next nine months I suffered the agonies of thirst and hunger; and even when the air turned disgustingly foul, I did not suffocate, though I ceased to be able to breathe. Down there in eternal darkness, with only the worms as companions, my mind altered its natural function. The loathsome book with which I had been buried began working upon me. The pitiful torment of being on the very threshold of dying, and yet not dying, of wishing above all else for an end to suffering and for oblivion, only to have oblivion snatched away, again and again, even though one knows it to be the sole remaining means of release! This endlessly recurring nightmare was my hideous fate. Darkness itself nurtured me. Alien words of hideous import coursed through the thoughts which were not my own, forcing mine back down into the rotten cellars housed deep within my brain. I had myself become a form of creeping contagion, a disease controlling my old mind, and all individual volition yielded to the dictates of collective infection and of ultimate degeneracy. Hell is not a physical place or even a state of being; hell is a certain occult system known solely to those initiated in the witch-cult: it is an active conspiracy which enthrones privation . . .

Nine months below ground in 1648.

The witch-finders dragged me from my grave. I heard them digging down towards my casket, the sound of their spades slicing into the earth, getting closer and closer as the excavation proceeded. Then there came the noise of muffled voices speaking in the accents and the idiom of my own age.

"Art thou certain this is the accursed spot?"

"Aye, Master. He was of the King's Party. He lies with his Fellows."

"Thou hast been in errour thrice before now."

"The entire Region is plaguey with Sorcerers. And 'tis He who commands them: I tell you, the Seventh Baron is not Dead."

"Was he not hanged by the Neck these Nine Months past?"

"Aye, and still all the Village murdered in their Beds."

The speakers scraped the soil away from the window-pane in the coffin lid and the burst of maddening sunlight caused me to flinch at its sheer intensity. It seemed to bore into my very skull; the enemy of darkness was again in the ascendant.

"Behold its Face of Crimson and its staring Eyes! The Face of the Devill. The Hands like Spiders. I told thee no lye. Lord Saul lives: see, even now he stirs."

One of the interlopers, a Roundhead soldier, removed the coffin-lid and shroud, and unceremoniously hauled me out on-to the side of the grave, where I writhed and cursed in the ap-palling sunshine. My supreme powers appeared to have deserted me in this dazzling universe of illumination, and it was all I could do just to take in my surroundings through squinting eyes that bubbled and boiled with blood. I saw the grim-set faces of three other men: Puritans in capotains and capes, their black garb and boots speckled by brown earth. Above lurked a cavernous blue sky. I tried to conceal the book with my long white hands and fingers, but to no avail.

"Witness it: there, 'tis still clutched to his Bosom—the Boke of Names and Spells wherein all his Confederates hath made their Mark in Blood."

"Fetch the foule Bastard and his damn'd Boke to the Pyre."

Then they dragged me up the hillside, towards the summit of the hill, and I was cursed and spat upon by gawking peasant-ry, those ignorant day-dwellers, who had gathered outside the shunned burial-ground in order to watch the spectacle. And upon that hill-summit there stood a wooden stake erected in the middle of a huge pile of chopped wood. There they bound me fast and I saw—through eyes now streaming blood—that the day could not last much longer, for the dying sun was turning a shade of crimson, mimicking the colour of my own face, and the night would soon be triumphant again.

"Light the Pyre, lest all be lost! We must be away before Nightfall."

The Roundhead stepped forward with a blazing torch in his hand, brought up a glob of sputum from the back of his throat and spat it directly into my face.

"Thou hast destroyed thyself, Wizzard, and thyself hath brought this greatest of miseries upon thee," he said, while he lit the faggots.

As the flames took hold and crackled their searing way up along my twitching, agonised limbs, blackening my hair, my flesh, and my Royalist cavalier garb, but merely singeing the leather boards of the book pressed against my heart by the imperishable white hands, I turned my unflinching gaze to the horizon, for darkness was approaching and its heralds of shadow gradually crept across the fields.

Once the sun had ultimately set and its rosy afterglow had faded utterly, and once all the day-dwellers had dispersed—they having thought me dead for a second time but also fearing mightily the nightfall—only then did the red-lichen-mottled gargoyles, hunchbacked and snouted and howling a chorus in unison as of old, gather about me, release me from bondage, and take me down off the stake in the middle of the still-smoking embers of the pyre.

And the teratological monsters ferried my now maimed and flame-blackened body, with the still-intact book clasped to my bosom, back through the gates outside space and time into the night-haunted and eternal tomb that is Thool Abbey of the latter Lammas—whence I was never again to depart.

And in those endlessly chanting rooms, and in the dreams of the blind, and in the penmanship of a left hand as white as its right twin, my heritage was finally restored and immortal renown achieved in the depths of Gehenna.

So it is written, so shall it be.

www.ingramcontent.com/pod-product-compliance
Lightning Source LLC
Chambersburg PA
CBHW071944170626
46813CB00005B/1821